IN THE
BELLY OF THE
BELL-SHAPED
CURVE

MICHAEL CARTER

IN THE BELLY OF THE BELL-SHAPED CURVE

iUniverse books may be ordered through booksellers or by contacting:

iUniverse
1663 Liberty Drive
Bloomington, IN 47403
www.iuniverse.com
844-349-9409

ISBN: 978-1-6632-0684-8 (sc)
ISBN: 978-1-6632-0686-2 (hc)
ISBN: 978-1-6632-0685-5 (e)

Library of Congress Control Number: 2020914798

Print information available on the last page.

iUniverse rev. date: 12/11/2020

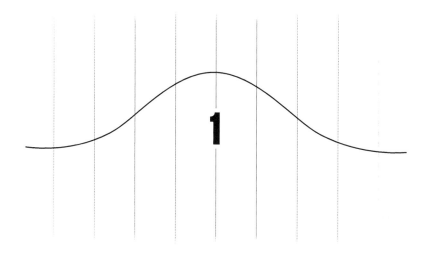

1

"Your ad said we would never have to work again."

"That's exactly right!" Turk said. "Your monkey does the work. Your monkey makes the money. All you have to do is take care of your monkey!"

"Okay. So what I think you're saying is that you don't actually have any monkeys for sale today, but if we give you some of our money now to invest in this idea of yours, we stand to make a lot of money in the future. We will also be guaranteed our own free Primo ... something, whatever you call them, these chimpanzees that do all the work—"

"Primo-Primates. And I must say, not only is this a great investment opportunity, but it is, perhaps, the beginning of an entirely new way of life!"

It was nine o'clock Monday morning. Turk was huddled in the corner of a fast-food restaurant with three middle-aged men who had responded to his ad in the local paper. He was wearing aviator sunglasses with mirrored lenses, knowing they could not see his eyes, only their own reflections staring back at them. Turk thought this was a great sales technique.

The tabletops were shiny and resilient. The tables were molded into the chairs, which were bolted to the floor. The walls were only three feet high and painted to look like red bricks. Mounted above was a continuous panel of thick glass. The entire dining area could be hosed down, wiped clean, and disinfected in minutes. Turk and his colleagues were enclosed in a safe, hermetically sealed environment.

As Turk looked down at his small audience, it occurred to him that, unfortunately, he was very much among his peers. They all looked older, fatter, and balder than how he saw himself, but he knew that he could no longer cover up the signs of aging. He had the inevitable roll of fat around his waistline that his suit coat could no longer hide and the beginnings of a double chin. His cheeks were slightly flushed and a little puffy. He still had his hair, most of it, but it was turning from brown to gray. He kept it cut short, but the gray parts stuck out straighter than the rest.

Although Turk sensed skepticism from his questioner, he stood firm. The key was to exude confidence. There was no way he could convince others to believe in his revolutionary concept if they were not convinced that he believed in it. As he spoke, he made emphatic gestures with his right hand. In his left hand, he held a large Styrofoam cup filled with steaming hot coffee.

"Think about it," continued Turk. "You could sit around in your underwear and monitor your investments. You could play computer games or poker online all day. You could paint or write poetry. You could eat potato chips, lie by the pool, and have a beer, watch TV, whatever you want. No more work for you. The monkeys do all the work. Utopia! A Trotskian paradise!"

Turk waited for a reaction, but there was no response.

"Here's the thing. I could operate this entire restaurant with only one human being. You wouldn't believe what scientists are doing with chimpanzees. They're teaching them how to communicate in sign language, how to operate simple machinery, even how to play video games. We all know that in the early days of the space program, they launched chimps into space. Our primate cousins were actually the first to explore outer space."

Turk paused for a moment. He realized he was talking too loud and too fast. He often did this when he got excited. He had tried to work on it. Liz, his now ex-wife, used to tell him to calm down and stop quacking like a duck. Don't talk *at* people, she would say, talk *to* them.

"So how do you plan to pull this off? Why are you asking us for money to help fund a project involving a bunch of monkeys?"

It was the same guy who had asked the previous questions. Turk knew from experience that if he could convince this guy, the dominant one, the other two would follow his lead. Turk had learned at least this much from his research on primates. But this guy was a total assclown. What Turk had not learned from his research was whether being the dominant one also meant being an arrogant asshole, or at least an asshole. The guy had gray stubble on his face, and his hair looked greasy and disheveled. His shirt was wrinkled. If he was so smart, why was he sitting here on a Monday morning in a fast-food restaurant responding to Turk's ad?

"At this moment, I'm in negotiations with my contacts in Africa to purchase the chimpanzees. I'm developing software to operate cash registers that make it even easier for the chimps to do simple transactions. Even with the technology that is now available, you don't have to be able to add and subtract, just count from one to ten. The computer tells you how much change to give back to the customer. I'm developing manuals that will show, step-by-step, how to train the chimps to operate these machines.

"I've got a business plan that combines advanced chimpanzee training techniques to enhance animal intelligence with computer technology that simplifies the most basic, boring, and mundane tasks that we humans engage in. You have a once-in-a-lifetime chance to be in on the ground floor of something truly revolutionary. This is an opportunity that comes along maybe once in a millennium. This is not just a product but the foundation of an ideology that will redefine the entire concept of work. You pay us a small fee upfront, and we train your monkey, well actually, chimpanzee. We train the chimp to do your job. The monkey takes your place and does your job for you. The monkey does the work. The monkey makes the money. All you have to do is take care of your monkey!"

Turk realized again that he was talking too loudly and had started flailing his right hand wildly. He looked around the restaurant to make sure he had not drawn attention to himself.

"So how much do these monkeys cost?" asked the assclown.

"Well, you're one step ahead of me here. We don't actually have the chimps yet. That's why we are looking for investors—farsighted men and women who can make this concept a reality, people who are willing to put down a small amount of money now for potentially huge profits in the future. The potential market is as large as the population of the planet. Everyone will want their own surrogate worker to do as much for them as possible.

"There is a definite market here. I mean, who wants to do all this boring, menial shit day in and day out? I don't. Do you? I've found a truly primal need and developed a plan to fill that need. This is something that men and women have yearned for throughout all human history. It is embedded deep in our collective consciousness. It is the desire to be free from work! It is the hope that someday we can be free from the boring and menial tasks that drag us down and make us dread our day-to-day existence."

"So the bottom line is that you are asking us for money now, but we don't know when we will ever get our chimps?" the assclown said sarcastically.

"Not exactly," replied Turk. "What we're talking about is *investing* your money with the expectation of increasing your wealth. And, of course, once you have realized a huge profit from your investment, you'll be able to buy all the chimps that you want."

"I thought your ad said come to this seminar and we would never have to work again."

"That's right. That's what we're talking about. Take care of your monkey."

"The ad didn't say anything about investing. It talked about making money without working." The assclown wouldn't let it go.

"Right, but not immediately, not in the short term. We have to take a slightly broader view." Turk paused. "This is probably a good time to take a break. I promised you breakfast. I'll tell you what. Here's a twenty-dollar bill. You guys go ahead and buy yourselves anything you want. And if there's any change left over, keep it. You've all got my business card. If this sounds like something you'd be interested in pursuing, give me a call or shoot me an email."

As the two men and the assclown moved from the table to the counter to order their complimentary breakfasts, Turk felt a twinge of frustration. He had to remember what he had learned from countless self-help compact discs and books. He could not look on this as a setback. He was now three people closer to finding an investor. He had ruled out these bozos. They weren't worth any more of his time.

On the other side of the thick glass, standing within just a few feet of Turk, a man was cleaning the outside of the window with a squeegee. Turk had not noticed him, and he didn't seem to have noticed Turk. The man could not have heard the speech that Turk had made to the others inside the glass. Although standing in plain sight on the opposite side of the transparent wall, Turk felt invisible to him. They could be living in the same instant in parallel dimensions. The man outside could not possibly smell the coffee and frying grease inside. Behind him, the sky was clear blue. At the edge of the parking lot there was a single tree on a strip of grass surrounded by concrete. It was late August, but Turk could not feel the heat and humidity outside. Inside the glass, the temperature was always perfect, always the same. No allergens could creep in. His sinuses were safe for now.

Turk pressed the accelerator to the floor as he turned onto the entrance ramp to the interstate. In an instant, he was up to speed and merged seamlessly into the flow of traffic. He was driving the economy car provided by his employer, a national insurance company. As a claims adjuster, his job involved investigating and settling personal injury and property damage claims, mostly automobile accidents. He had tried sales once for a brief stint but went back to claims. The money was not as good, but it was steady and he got a company car.

Although the office hours were eight thirty to five, Turk wasn't worried about being late to work. His job often took him out of the office. He had covered himself by logging an entry into the global office calendar, indicating that he had an appointment to take a recorded statement from a claimant. No one would expect him in until late morning. This was one of the tricks he had learned over the years. Contemporaneous false documentation and revisionist documentation of past events could be powerful tools in creating a false reality that allowed him to do less while appearing to meet the company's expectations.

Though the deception troubled him occasionally because Turk thought of himself as a moral person, it was necessary to give him more time to work on his PPP, his Primo-Primate Project, that would someday improve and enhance his life and the lives of countless human beings and their primate cousins. In pursuit of such a noble cause, in this limited set of circumstances, the ends justified the means.

Turk worked for the American Security Casualty and Assurance Corporation, but he was actually employed by a subsidiary of that corporation, American Security Services, or ASS, as he referred to it. Some insurance companies allowed their adjusters to work from home. American Security required their claims *representatives* to work from the office. He would have preferred to work from home but still got out enough that he was able to pursue his outside ventures, one of which he hoped would make him rich someday.

He could retire early. All he would have to do was take care of his monkey.

He inserted one of his favorite compact discs into the stereo. It was his favorite band from the days of his youth: Felix Frankfurter and the Psychomatics. Turk cranked up the volume. The cheap speakers in his company car couldn't handle it. They started vibrating wildly and distorting the sound. This made the music even better. Felix's voice was deep and rich. The bass guitar throbbed. It was one of Turk's favorite songs: "Badass!" Felix attacked the upper register of his electric guitar and screeched out a high riff that sliced deep into Turk's inner ears. The drummer pounded so hard that the beat threatened to overpower the normal rhythm of Turk's heart and shock it into sync with the ancient primal rhythms.

Felix, like so many other rock stars of his era, had died young after living a life of excess and glory. After his death, it was discovered that he had written volumes of philosophical treatises in addition to his music. He became a cult figure and one of the heroes of Turk's life. His hard-core followers professed to believe that he was the third incarnation of the ancient Greek god Dionysus.

Turk could remember the first time he heard one of Felix's albums. He had been in his dorm room his freshman year of college, smoking dope and getting high with friends. His roommate had showed up to college with huge speakers, which, at the time, were considered to have a high quality of resonance. As the music had intensified, Turk had sat back on the couch, laid his head against the cushion, and closed his eyes.

The sound had been overpowering. But in that moment, Turk hadn't just heard the music. He had *seen* the music. He could see the different colors of the notes. He could see a light show exploding in his mind. He had focused on the third eye on his forehead, just above and between his two eyes. In an instant, he had shot light-years ahead into infinity, into the space-time continuum, into a broader connection to the universe, and all this without ever having practiced meditation.

Somehow, Felix had the ability to open up vast new areas of Turk's awareness and consciousness. He was fortunate to have had the opportunity to attend one of the last concerts Felix performed before his unfortunate and untimely death.

Then came the rumors that perhaps Felix wasn't really dead but had faked his death to escape the pressure of the fame that had blown his life out of proportion. Some called for his grave to be excavated and his casket opened to determine if he was buried there. This had not happened. When Turk had learned of the discovery of Felix's writings, he had gone online and downloaded what he thought would someday be considered sacred texts.

The first one was titled "Agape." Once Turk had read that treatise, he'd been hooked. He continued to listen to Felix's music and read everything he could find that Felix had written, and also hoped that, if Felix were still alive, someday he might encounter him.

Mondays were the worst. Not only did Turk lose a good chunk of Sunday evening dreading it, but once it arrived, he was locked in for five days. Sure, there was a little time off each night before he went to bed, just enough time to eat, run errands, and worry about the next day.

Today would be especially bad. He had a meeting with his new boss, Allen S. Smith, who had been the claims manager at a branch office and had just been promoted to regional claims manager. He had scheduled appointments with all the adjusters to "get acquainted." Turk's meeting was scheduled for eleven thirty. He was dreading the encounter.

Smith had a reputation for being both a tight-ass and an ass-kisser to upper management, which could only make Turk's life more difficult. In his first staff meeting last Friday, Smith had stated emphatically, "If we don't owe it, then we won't pay a dime! And if all that we owe is a dime, we won't pay a penny more!" This, of course, was what Smith's bosses wanted to hear. Be aggressive. Protect the bottom line. Maximize profits for the company by wringing out the wasted dollars paid out on illegitimate claims. But for Turk and the other subordinates in the office, this meant only that they would have to work harder and be subject to greater scrutiny.

Although he had not yet had a one-on-one conversation with the man, Turk had already formed his impression. He knew the type. He had seen it too many times. They claimed to be into the principle of the thing, whatever that was, but Turk knew it was something more egotistical. Smith was on his way up. This was just one more step toward his next promotion. He looked good on the reports. Upper management loved him, but the people underneath loathed him.

Guys like Smith represented what Turk hated most: he was all about himself and the advancement of his career. He would come in vowing to clean up the department and show his superiors what he had accomplished. He would have no concern for those who worked for him, only that they met the metrics Turk was sure Smith would put into place. If not, they would be out. Smith didn't see them as people with families and the need to support themselves. He just expected them to kick out the work and meet the arbitrary expectations he would impose. And the worst part of it would be that he would not really have a good grasp of their jobs, the nuances and intricacies. He would be focused only on results as he defined them, and ultimately, clouded by his own self-interest, he would probably be a concrete thinker. So he would buy in to whatever he perceived his bosses expected. Once guys like that were programmed, every time the bell rang, they salivated like one of Pavlov's dogs.

What made it especially frustrating for Turk was that he knew he could have gone that route. He had been offered a supervisor's job back when he was only about five years into the business but had turned it down. He liked the freedom of being an adjuster and hated being chained to a desk. But maybe that decision had been a mistake. Maybe he had foreclosed any possibility that he would ever be considered for a promotion again. Maybe, in one principled but silly move, he had placed a cap on his future income potential. Perhaps that was the decision that had started the chain of events that had ultimately ended in his ex-wife, Liz, filing for divorce.

Growing up, he had never dreamed of being a claims adjuster. But that was what he had become. And he believed that his job defined him and who he was in the eyes of others. Being a claims adjuster wasn't impressive or sexy or lucrative, but it also wasn't bad. It was an average and perfectly respectable white-collar occupation for a college graduate. He should have been able to be content with his station in life.

But that wasn't enough for him. And he knew Liz had sensed his frustration. If he wasn't happy with his life and what he had become, how could he expect her to be happy with him? She hadn't signed up for that. And Turk got it. But he still missed the life they'd had as an intact family living together in the same home, when he could wake up every morning and be with his kids. He also missed Liz, as annoying as she could be sometimes with her continual stream of do-it-yourself projects. All in all, despite the disagreements and ensuing arguments, he had wanted to try and work it out, but she wouldn't even try marriage counseling.

What worried Turk the most about Smith now, however, was that a guy like him might be just smart enough, and anal enough, to figure out Turk's scams and his true lack of productivity on his job. Over many years of adjusting claims, he had figured out the shortcuts and duplication of previous work that made his job easy. He had learned how to manage and evade the bogus deadlines, how to keep the endless forms and reports flowing, and how to comply with the company's arbitrary reporting guidelines. It was form that mattered, not substance. All he had to do was meet most of the deadlines, get some type of report in by the due date, regardless of the content, even if the report said only that he would be sending a full report later, and that was good enough to get by. And in so doing, he received consistently average, and sometimes above average, job performance evaluations from his superiors. That translated into steady, although modest, raises and the minimal job security that came with the slow accumulation of time spent in one place.

Turk was living a double life, like a secret agent. He was one person in his work life, his responsible adult life, but his true, dynamic self was the person who would pull off the PPP and change the world for the better. He had to make time for what was truly important in the long term, beyond just the day-to-day. He sometimes wondered if Liz had ever appreciated that part of him. He couldn't accept the possibility that she left him because she thought he was a schlub.

A new boss injected an element of uncertainty into Turk's domain all right. Was Smith sharp enough to figure out just how little work Turk had been doing on his job as he worked endlessly to develop his outside ventures? Would Smith finally discover what a truly worthless claims adjuster and, by extension, human being he really was? Had Smith talked to Liz?

"Good morning," said Smith.

They shook hands. Contrary to Turk's expectation, Smith's grip was limp. He was tall and slender with medium length, perfectly groomed dark hair. He wore a pressed white shirt with a maroon tie. Turk knew that Smith had attended an Ivy League college out east, and as Turk expected, Smith exuded that stereotypical prep school aura. Turk sat down in the chair across from Smith's desk. On the front was a nameplate that read, Allen S. Smith, Executive Vice President and Regional Claims Manager.

"Well, the reason I called you here is that I wanted to meet personally with all my new staff. I think this type of 'face-to-face' is invaluable. You get to know me a little, and I get to know you."

"I think that is an excellent way to begin, sir," said Turk.

"Now you have to understand that to be a good manager, although I would love to do it, I can't always be buddy-buddy with my staff."

"I understand."

"Bill, I've had a chance to look at your personnel file," said Smith. Turk's legal name was William Malone, so Smith must have assumed that Turk went by the name Bill. And actually, Smith was correct. Turk was a nickname he'd been tagged with in college. Even Liz called him Bill. But in his own mind, he still thought of himself as Turk, even though he hadn't talked with any of his college buddies in years.

"You are one of our more experienced adjusters. And I'd have to say that definitely, without question, you are at least average, or maybe even a little better."

"Thank you, sir," responded Turk.

"Your reports are a little brief, but they're adequate."

"Thank you."

"The way you stay on top of things is above average, and it appears that you relate well to the claimants. And that's important. You establish that rapport. They get to trust you. It usually results in a cheaper settlement."

"I agree."

"So then the question becomes," continued Smith, "how does *Bill* raise his level of play, make himself stand out in this organization? How does Bill rise above the mediocre and make himself a true asset to this company?"

There was a long pause. Smith settled back in his chair, looked Turk directly in the eye, and waited for a response.

"Well," Turk said finally, "I suppose *Bill* ... could start by asking his new boss for any suggestions that he might have as to how Bill could improve his performance."

"Good answer!" said Smith, springing up in his chair and flipping his index finger at Turk and then into the air as if he had just shot a bullet from a pistol. "I turned things around in my previous position, and I can do it here. And Bill can be an integral part of this process. Bill can listen to me. Even if he doesn't always understand why I'm doing certain things, it will become evident later. Bill can implement these things. Bill can be a team player. Bill can work harder. Bill can strive to be the best Bill that Bill can be!"

Turk's initial visceral response was a desire to reach across the desk, grab this little punk by the throat, and scream into his face,

"How did you ever get to be so fucking stupid!" Instead, Turk used a trick he had learned from one of his favorite self-help CDs, *How to Keep from Losing Your Head and Blaming It on Your Mother.*

He drew a deep breath and paused for a moment to reflect on the situation. The trick was to detach and watch the events as if he were an outside observer looking in. He watched himself. He watched Smith. He considered Smith's motivations. He contemplated the absurdity of the situation in the overarching scheme of things. He contemplated the ultimate insignificance to Smith of his feelings or ego or his revolutionary plans for changing the world. He realized that what was coming out of Smith's mouth revealed more about Smith than it did about himself.

"I understand what you're saying," Turk said. "I'll do just what you said. And I'll do it to the best of my ability."

"Good. I'm glad to see that you are on board. Okay. I guess we've covered the positive things. Now comes the part of the job I don't particularly like. I told you in the beginning that to be effective, I can't be buddy-buddy with everyone."

"Yes, you did."

"And that means I can't always be Mr. Popularity around here."

"Yes."

"So now we need to get specific. What is that first thing Bill can do better?"

Turk paused again. "I'm not really sure. But I would love to hear your constructive suggestions so that I can try to implement them into my daily work routine."

"Well," said Smith. "First of all, we'd like to see you around this office a little more. I know face-to-face contact with claimants is good, but consider the lost travel time. My suggestion is that before you schedule an appointment outside the office, every time you pick up a file, ask yourself, 'Is there a more efficient way that Bill can handle this? Can I take care of this with a phone call or a short letter? Is there any part of this task that Bill can delegate to the office staff?' Do you see what I'm getting at?"

Turk was now into full-blown detachment mode. He could see the absurdity of the situation, and because of his broader awareness, he could choose to play along but was not bound by the rules of the game. But who had tipped Smith off about Turk needing to spend more time in the office?

"Absolutely!" Turk said. "And I'll do exactly what you just said. That is such a helpful recommendation. I can see how that simple suggestion could increase Bill's productivity. It could change how Bill conducts his daily activities of living. It could change Bill's life!"

Turk suddenly realized that he was talking too loudly again. He felt a slight twinge of panic. He did not want to lose control. He drew another deep breath and went back into detachment mode. Smith smiled and nodded, apparently pleased with himself that he had offered such brilliant advice.

"I'm glad to hear that," said Smith. "I can see that you and I are going to get along just fine. Now, another thing. And this is not directed at you. It appears there are some adjusters in this office who tend to overpay claims just to get rid of them. And I know that sometimes it can't be helped. But a pattern of this sort of thing, well, that can really add up. Then our figures look bad compared to the other regional offices. I'm trying to get to the bottom of this. I'm sure you see what a problem this can be."

"Of course."

"You know, we audit files and look for these sorts of things, look for red flags."

"Uh-huh."

"I've got my suspicions. But it's not always easy to spot, especially with the more experienced ones. And I'm new here. Soon enough, I'll have a good handle on this. I will be implementing metrics to track the number of claims received by each adjuster, the timeliness of their reports, the time between opening and closing a file, the amount paid to settle a claim in relation to the amount of medical bills incurred by the claimant—these types of information. But in the short term, I know you've been around for a while and are yourself an experienced adjuster. Could you help point us in the right direction?"

Turk was thrust out of detachment mode and back into the present moment. He felt his cheeks flush, which often happened when he was under stress or had drunk too much alcohol. He tried not to glare across the desk as his anger intensified. This last ploy was especially diabolical. Smith had just arrived, and he was already trying to drive a wedge between the adjusters, develop a mole so he could have a pipeline to inside information about his underlings. There was a time when Turk might have given in to his passions, lost control, let loose with his real emotions, and blurted out the words bouncing around in his brain: *You'll never fool ol' Turk with this bullshit! I'm not your buddy! You're a punk! You're an anal-retentive, gold-plated asshole!*

Turk took another deep breath. The momentary satisfaction was not worth what he stood to lose. Life, after all, was a continual series of compromises.

"Well, I'm sorry, but *Bill* really doesn't know what you're talking about. I know I always try to pay what's fair and not one penny more."

"Well, what's fair often depends on your point of view," said Smith.

Smith shrugged and raised his eyebrows slightly as he looked Turk directly in the eye. He seemed open and approachable, although Turk thought he could detect a subtle smirk on his face. Damn, this guy was good! Somehow he had used his superior position to manipulate the dynamic of the interaction and put the burden on Turk. They had just met, but already Turk had to choose sides. He had to either offer up some information to signal that he was a team player or put himself out there and brand himself as a potential troublemaker, a rogue adjuster. He had to either submit to Smith's will or place himself in a position where he would be under strict observation and scrutiny. Turk was not prepared for this encounter. He had underestimated his opponent.

Smith continued to stare while Turk wallowed in indecision. He knew he would not submit to Smith and provide him with any information, no matter how insignificant. His thoughts raced as he tried to find a way to get out of the encounter without a direct confrontation. The moment seemed to stretch on interminably.

Finally, the solution came to him: passive-aggression! The idea should have occurred to him immediately. Throughout his entire life, others had used it so effectively on him. He should be a master at it. He just needed to switch roles. His lack of response would be his response.

Turk resolved that he would not look away, even if he had to blink occasionally. In the meantime, as he embraced Smith in a mutual stare down, Smith continued to fix his gaze directly onto Turk's eyes. But Turk was now in it for the long haul. He could wait the guy out. Fortunately, he didn't have to piss, which could possibly have affected his stamina. Smith kept staring at him, and he kept staring back. He had no idea how long this went on. The moment was suspended in time.

Smith slowly tightened his eyelids to the point that he was squinting at Turk with a steely, reptilian glare. Then he slowly nodded as if he had drawn a conclusion about something, probably something negative about Turk.

Turk responded by squinting his eyelids and focusing his stare, laser-like, on Smith's left eye and only his left eye. Turk's gaze bore directly into the dark pupil of his opponent with an intensity that Turk believed penetrated straight into the back of Smith's skull. Smith briefly shifted glances between Turk's right and left eyes. Turk sat firm. He could sense Smith trying to reconnect, but it was too late. He had lost his position of dominance. This round went to Turk. He had refused to be intimidated and had managed to do so without giving Smith any objective reason to be upset with him. Still, after this encounter, Turk knew he could be a target. They were both, after all, descendants of their evolutionary past.

"Okay then," continued Smith. "I drafted a memo this morning. You should all have it by this afternoon. We are starting a new procedure. From this point forward, all requests for authority to settle any claims will go through me. I developed a new claims evaluation form. When you request settlement authority, you will fill out this separate executive summary memorandum and attach it to the standard liability/settlement evaluation report. I'll be reviewing these forms closely. I need to get a handle on what's going on here. My goal is to have the lowest payout per claim of any regional office in the country and the highest percentage of claim files closed within six months after receipt of the claim."

Turk nodded politely. He had to control the urge to break into a haughty grin. A new report form was sure to solve all of Smith's perceived problems with this office. Turk stood up to leave. "Are we finished then?"

"One more thing," Smith said. "As I said, I will be instituting metrics in this office, processes to measure performance, increase accountability, improve quality, and obtain better outcomes. With your years of experience, I think you could provide valuable input into measurements we could design to capture this important information."

Metrics! Even though Turk had expected it, Smith had almost regained the dominate position in a millisecond. Damn, this guy was good! Asking Turk to design metrics to measure his performance was like asking him to dig his own grave. But wait, maybe this was a good thing. Now he knew for sure what Smith was up to. Now he was on the inside. Yes, he would provide valuable input. But since Smith was so clueless about the details of Turk's job, he wouldn't understand that Turk's input would be at cross-purposes to what he wanted.

"I've thought that this should have been done for years!" responded Turk. "Yes, I can definitely provide you with significant valuable input." He was back on top.

"Okay," said Smith. "This is a project we will be implementing in about six months. I'll let you know. And I look forward to hearing your suggestions at that time."

"Thank you, sir," Turk said. "It was nice to meet you, and Bill looks forward to using this new evaluation form and providing you valuable insight into the new metrics that you'll be designing."

As Turk drove home that evening, he decided it was time to cross the line and do whatever was necessary, legal or illegal, although not immoral in his view. He couldn't handle it anymore. He was barely making his child support payments. He had accumulated massive credit card debt. He was standing on the precipice of a financial black hole. The irony was that the more he borrowed, the more credit card offers he received. He assumed it was because he never missed a minimum payment. He had an excellent credit rating. So it seemed his ability to borrow was nearly unlimited as long as he was able to keep making those minimum monthly payments.

Now he was stuck as he struggled to make each monthly payment when it was due and his debt increased as he continued to live beyond his means. He had no realistic possibility of paying it off in the foreseeable future unless he was successful in pulling off the PPP. He had fallen for their scheme. They had him by the balls.

He had never done anything illegal. He wasn't sure if he was psychologically or emotionally equipped to be a criminal, even a nonviolent white-collar one. He always felt an underlying sense of unease about everything. Once he had actually broken the law, would he be constantly looking over his shoulder?

But after years of adjusting claims, he thought he had come up with an embezzlement scheme that would be undetectable: Turk's perfect claim. His plan was to set up a fictitious claimant with a complete claim file, bogus medical bills, a false identity, a phony transcript of a recorded statement—everything. He would then settle the claim with this fictitious person. The real money generated from this settlement, however, would be deposited into Turk's real bank account.

He wouldn't cause any harm to a real person. He would simply be taking back some of the money that American Security should have been paying him over the years, or money it wasted by paying inflated salaries to guys like Smith. And the best part of his scheme was that he would use the new executive summary memorandum to get Mr. Allen S. Smith, executive vice president and regional claims manager, his new *best bud Smitty,* to authorize the bogus settlement.

Turk, of course, did not plan to spend any of the settlement money on himself, but would use that money to purchase the chimps that he would use to revolutionize the world and hopefully bring an end to the monotony, boredom, and meaninglessness of so many lives, and ultimately, the stigma of mediocrity. After he had achieved this goal, not just for himself but for the betterment of others, money and recognition were sure to follow.

Turk turned off of the interstate, glided smoothly onto the exit ramp, and then slowly descended into a maze of timed stoplights and interconnecting roads. To his right, he noticed that a construction company had just poured a new concrete sidewalk leading into a new office complex. After driving a few miles, he arrived at his subdivision. At the entrance, the city council had recently installed a stoplight. When he exited his subdivision each morning on his way to work, it was a constant source of frustration. The idiots had placed a No Right Turn on Red sign at the intersection, which meant Turk couldn't pull out into traffic when he saw an opening. Instead, he was forced to wait until the light turned green. Well, that wasn't going to happen. There were never any cops around. Turk wasn't a soldier dutifully obeying an order. So he blew through that red light every day.

After the divorce, Liz got both the house and the kids. And Turk was fine with that. He had agreed to all of it in the divorce settlement agreement. He wanted the best for his kids. But he still ached to see them more than just during his visitation times. And living alone was tough, although it gave him more time to work on his projects.

Turk had moved into an apartment for three months but could not tolerate the notion that he was one of the masses who got absolutely no return on their money, no equity, no appreciation, no tax deduction, nothing. So he had decided to take a chance in Emerald Forest. It was all he could afford. They were assembly-line homes. He had gotten to choose from among several options for the floor plan, size, color, cabinets, carpeting, and several other features. All the homes had brick on the front and aluminum siding on the back.

Turk's problem was that he should have checked out the developer and the location. There was a sewage treatment plant just half a mile north. It was usually no problem. However, when the wind blew from north to south, the stench was overpowering. Turk could not take a walk outside. He was forced to shut himself inside the house with the doors and windows closed. Still, the smell would creep in. There was no escape.

The builder had gone bankrupt before completing the project, so the neighborhood was left unfinished. Turk and a dozen other hapless homebuyers lived in new homes, with freshly paved streets and city water and sewer, but were surrounded by empty lots and roads that ended abruptly and led to nowhere but more empty, undeveloped lots. Turk had heard that another builder was interested in completing the project, but nothing had materialized. In the meantime, he knew he had no hope of selling his house for enough money to cover the cost of the mortgage. So at least for now, he was stuck.

Turk hit the remote to the garage door and pulled his car inside. He hit the remote again to close the door. He watched in the rearview mirror to make sure the door went all the way down and did not spring back up. He still had not gotten around to installing drywall to cover the bare upright two-by-fours. He entered the kitchen through the garage door and threw his keys on the counter.

He descended the stairs into the unfinished walkout basement. He opened the sliding glass doors and went onto the patio that opened to a small fenced-in backyard. He was tired, and his neck and shoulders were knotted up, but the heat was even more stifling.

When he entered the yard, Turk heard the incessant chirping sound and remembered it was time to water his crickets. He had placed a vat on the patio that comprised his cricket farm. If the developer had ever completed the neighborhood, this would probably have been a violation of the homeowners association's restrictive covenants. But after things went belly-up, Turk was no longer concerned. This little venture was already bringing in a small but steady stream of income. He was making inroads with the small bait-and-tackle shops in the city. The nearest cricket farm he knew of was at least an hour away, out in the country. But there were numerous places to fish in and around the city. He was the closest bait supplier, and the clients were pleased with his service.

If his other ideas did not catch on, this enterprise just might be his ticket out of the rut he was in, the routine that had become his daily existence, days that turned into weeks that turned into months that turned into years.

The breeding instructions were simple. There were virtually no start-up costs. All one needed was about fifty crickets, male and female; some topsoil; a mineral called vermiculite; and water, lots of water. That was easy for Turk to supply from the hose in his backyard.

He knew the underlying principle. He just needed to gut it out. Persevere. He closed his eyes and repeated his mantra: "The key is to find a need, then fill that need." And he hoped that once he completed his PPP, he would not only have found the need, but would also be able to implement his revolutionary changes to fill that need.

2

It was two o'clock in the morning. Turk was still awake. This was his time. This was when he made the most progress on his own projects. He had always had difficulty on both ends: falling asleep at night and waking up in the morning. So he had finally given up trying to fight it and settled into a routine of very little sleep at night and high doses of caffeine during the day. It was tough functioning on so little sleep, but his daily routine was so boring that he could sleepwalk through it. He couldn't reconcile his expectations and the mundane reality of his day-to-day existence without Liz and the kids to give meaning to the rut of work, money, and striving for who knows what.

He probably would have been happier if he had been born in a different time. If he had been born into a family in medieval times and his father was a blacksmith, he would probably have been able to accept his station in life and become a blacksmith. But he had been born in the land of opportunity. The promise of riches, and of a better, more exciting life, was omnipresent. It was on television, in magazines, and on the internet. He was constantly bombarded with the difference between this more glamorous and exciting way of life and his own. He focused obsessively on the idealized version of the person he could be but to whom he could never measure up.

He was in a constant, chronic state of cognitive dissonance. He couldn't bring harmony to the myriad thoughts and feelings spiraling out of sync and out of control in his mind. He had read plenty of self-help books that discussed the need for acceptance. But he couldn't accept it. He knew he wasn't alone, but somehow, the fact that most people lived such lives of desperation didn't ease his own pain and boredom.

During the summer between his sophomore and junior years in college, Turk had worked for a contractor who laid concrete and asphalt. That summer, his crew had poured dozens of parking lots, driveways, and sidewalks. His older coworkers had been part of the underbelly of society: divorced husbands, estranged fathers hopelessly behind in child support and dodging warrants, transients, ex-cons—all barely existing on the fringe of society, all getting by day-to-day on a cash-only basis.

Their names were irrelevant because they had numerous aliases, which often resembled their true names but had slight variances, like Edward Lee Jameson, a.k.a. James L. Edwards, a.k.a. Ed James, a.k.a. James E. Lee. They were mostly high school dropouts with little formal education, but they all knew how to pour concrete. A lot of the older ones had beer bellies and leathery sunbaked skin. Most of the younger guys were muscular, taut, and tattooed. They stayed out late at night drinking, fighting, and fucking. They didn't have enough foresight to use condoms, so unwanted offspring and disease were common. This was how they spent the twilight days of their youth.

Whenever he passed a construction project, he knew all the signs of freshly poured concrete. He knew to look for the yellow plastic strips placed to cordon off the area until it dried. On the way home that evening, he had spotted just such a place. The timing was right. Tonight, Turk would strike again. He had done it numerous times and never gotten caught, compelled by some impulse to leave his mark that he didn't completely understand. He also had a hammer and chisel that he used if he saw a good spot to leave his name in dried cement. This night played out like all the previous times.

He arrived at the scene around three o'clock in the morning. It was the new office complex he had passed on his way home earlier that evening. The concrete sidewalk had been poured earlier that afternoon. Turk turned off his headlights as he pulled into the parking lot. He drove around to the back of the building and parked his car on the perimeter of the lot. Using his flashlight, he walked to the site of the freshly laid concrete. It was still wet. He looked around in the darkness in every direction, checking for security cops.

He knelt down on his knees and pulled a screwdriver out of his back pocket. He then etched his name into the moist concrete slab— *Turk*. There it would remain for decades, perhaps even millennia. Maybe no one would ever notice it. Or maybe, in some distant moment, some little kid might stumble upon it, this insignificant detail in this insignificant time and place, and he—Turk—would have achieved maybe not immortality but at least one more distant yet fleeting instance where his existence would be acknowledged in the collective consciousness. And he would bear witness.

Thousands of years from now, would such a finding by some future archeologist be any less significant than the present-day discovery of primitive etchings uncovered among ancient ruins thousands of years old? At the time, weren't the inhabitants just ordinary primates like Turk? Turk was in it for the long haul. He had left his name in countless insignificant places, always sure to etch it deep into the concrete so that it would not wash away. For whatever it might be worth to posterity, Turk had left his mark.

He returned home. Now it was time to complete his ritual. He picked up his electric guitar but did not plug it into the amplifier. He imagined he was standing in front of a stadium full of adoring fans, like his idol, Felix. Turk wailed away frantically at his guitar strings, interspersing light riffs with heavy chords. Felix, like so many rock stars, had gotten incredibly rich off the minor pentatonic scale, even though only a few of his fans had any idea what it was.

Turk put the guitar down and started writing in his journal. He always typed it on the keyboard without turning on the computer. As dawn approached, he faced yet another meaningless, mind-numbingly boring day on the job, trying to function with no sleep on a caffeine-induced high but making money and fulfilling his responsibilities.

He pounded the keyboard furiously as he tried to document the details of his life. He wrote about the pain of loss and loneliness and unfulfilled dreams. He wrote about how he dreaded the upcoming day at work. He wrote about the oppressive financial child support he had to pay without getting enough time to actually be present with his kids. But he still had hopes and aspirations. He had a vision for a better future for himself and all humanoid kind. The PPP was the key. He had been beaten down, for sure, but they hadn't pounded out his ambition or his resilience. He had listened to enough self-help CDs that he knew that setbacks were to be expected. He had to pick himself back up and stay focused on his goals.

He hit the Ctrl-Alt not once but three times to make sure it was saved. He knew it would not be recorded here in this life. But somewhere in the universe, in some heavenly place, in some remote fold deep in the gray matter of God's infinite brain, this was being preserved. Exactly how this was being done, well, those were details for God to work out. But it would be there. There was no need to save it to the hard drive or print out a copy.

3

When Turk arrived at his house after work the next evening, he grabbed a frozen fish dinner from the freezer and put it into the microwave. When it finished cooking, he took his meal with him into his home office, which was adjacent to his kitchen and living room, and sat down at the desk. He had set up the office complete with a computer, copy machine, and printer.

He knew he would have to be meticulous in both the planning and execution of his embezzlement scheme. All the minor details would have to fit together perfectly, something he never had to worry about when he deceived his supervisors about how much, or rather how little, he worked. His past deceptions had been good practice. He had learned a few tricks. This time, however, he would be playing at a much higher level with potentially grave consequences. He was raising his game to an entirely new dimension.

It would not be that difficult. This new claimant would have a name very similar to his, with a social security number also very close to his, and the same date of birth. Turk went to the bank often. He was on a first name basis with most of the young men and women who worked there. He could easily fudge the names and numbers of his fictional claimant to match his own and in the process collect the settlement that his best bud *Smitty* would approve.

The reason his scheme should work was simple. It was based on the one universal, immutable, but often overlooked trait of human behavior: incompetence. No one would pay close attention. The people who would process the transaction would be as bored with their jobs as he was with his, and they wouldn't focus on the mundane little details. They would be sloppy, lazy, and careless.

As a claims adjuster, Turk had become an expert in the infinite variety of ways that people could screw up. He had witnessed the numerous ways people could cause physical injury and pain to others by mere carelessness. Whether they were working or driving or raising children, humans were inept. That was why someone at some point in history had found a need to provide insurance and then found a way to fill that need. That was why Turk had a job.

He had seen it all: people running red lights, people slipping on icy sidewalks, dentists giving vaginal exams, surgeons operating on the wrong limb. Sometimes there were screwups on multiple levels, like the case he had handled where the doctor removed the patient's good kidney by mistake and left her with the diseased one. She was pissed off, and so was her husband, so they sued. Then the lawyer who handled the medical malpractice case screwed up by forgetting to file the lawsuit within the two-year statute of limitations. He blew it by one day. So they sued him too.

Turk's immediate need was about $80,000 to $90,000. This would give him the seed money to start his grand enterprise: the PPP, the historic mind meld between chimpanzees and machines, the creation of an entirely new underclass of highly trained chimps that could operate computer software so sophisticated in design that any idiot could do it.

This was perhaps the next step in human history. He referred to it as the unintended consequence of the calculator. Undoubtedly, a great understanding of math had gone into the development of the calculator. But once this tool was created, those who used it did not need to be good at math anymore. While some would soar to new heights, the masses could do just what Turk had done—become gradually dependent on the technology and let his brain atrophy. He could hardly remember how to do long division on his own.

To come up with the $80K to $90K, his fictional claimant would need to have sustained a serious injury. A broken ankle would be good. He had handled lots of these over the course of his career. Medical bills were high. One had to undergo surgery and have hardware inserted. That was all very expensive. There would be a lot of pain and suffering, and his fictional claimant would inevitably develop arthritis in the joint. That would be worth even more money. Yet it was not a loss of limb or some catastrophic injury that would attract attention and be reviewed by the higher-ups in the home office.

He opened a file that he had closed just a few months ago. The claimant had fallen off a ladder on the insured's property and had broken his ankle. It was all there—medical bills, a report from the treating doctor, an impairment rating. He could simply change the names and other identifying information and use the reports and evaluations he had already prepared. All that would be required were a few manipulations in the company's internal processes in setting up new claims and some subtle forgery.

First, he had to come up with a name for his new person that was close enough to his own that he could slip it past the bank teller when he deposited the check from American Security into his own account. Turk's full name was William V. Malone. He would call this new being William W. Mahone. Those names could easily be confused when scribbling a quick signature. Turk would also give Mahone a social security number identical to his own, but with the two middle digits reversed.

As to the medical bills and reports, he would make copies; white out and retype the name, social security number, and other identifying information; and then recopy the forged documents. He would do the same with the transcript of Mr. Mahone's recorded statement that was in the file. After several copies, any noticeable differences would fade. This would serve as the underlying documentation in case anyone ever checked for accuracy, which would never happen, unless perhaps he got caught.

The most satisfying part, besides duping Smitty, would be using the company's elaborate reporting system to create this alternate reality. By embracing that which he hated most, he would be able to transcend the process and, once free, manipulate and control the outcome. All the supervisors ever saw were the reports. This incident, which would never actually happen, would exist as a real file among the company's vast number of claims being processed for accidents that had actually happened, injuries that had actually been sustained, and suffering that had actually occurred.

The hardest part would be the initial stage of reporting the claim and getting a file set up within the company's claim department. Turk knew intimately the minute details of how this process worked. When a policy holder, also called the insured, was involved in an accident, the insured would call his or her agent, who would then call in the report to the claims office, and a file would be set up. The case would be automatically assigned to the adjuster who handled that particular territory, who, in turn, would contact the claimant and handle the case to conclusion.

The adjuster would investigate the case, compile the documentation, and send a report to the supervisor with an evaluation of whether the insured was at fault, the seriousness of the injury, the amount of money necessary to compensate the claimant for the damages sustained, and the recommended settlement range of the claim. If the policyholder was not at fault, the adjuster would recommend that the claim be denied. If the adjuster determined that the insured was at fault, also referred to as negligent, the adjuster would request settlement authority, which was the upper limit of money the supervisor would authorize the adjuster to offer to the claimant to try and settle the case and avoid a lawsuit.

Buried in his closed files, Turk had policy information on hundreds of insureds. He also had access to the company's computer database that contained the names and policy information on all policyholders, as well as their claims history. All he needed to do was find a policyholder with no prior expensive claims; call that person's insurance agent, pretending to be that policyholder; and report that there had just been an accident involving a William W. Mahone. The agent would send that information to the claims office. A file would be set up. A few people might glance at the report, but they would not review it carefully. Turk would give Mr. Mahone an address in his territory, and the office would assign the case to Turk to handle.

He searched his database of old files until he found a promising candidate: Mr. John Brock. He had been involved in a minor rear-end accident the previous year. He had bumped the guy in the rear. There had been minimal property damage. The claimant had gone to the emergency room, where x-rays were done, and was diagnosed with a neck strain. He had followed up with his family doctor one time. After reading this, Turk remembered the case. Turk had paid to have the car repaired and settled the personal injury part of the claim for the cost of the medical bills and an extra hundred dollars for pain and suffering. The guy had been happy with the hundred bucks. He hadn't known he could have squeezed more money out of the accident.

Turk entered Brock's policy number into the company's computer database. Brock also carried his homeowner's insurance with American Security. Yes! He had the one minor fender bender on his record, which was the claim Turk had handled. Otherwise, there were no other claims. He had found the perfect insured.

American Security had a "no consent" policy, which meant that the company could settle a claim without the permission of the insured. This would make it easier for Turk to carry out his plan, but there was still a risk that if he settled a claim on Brock's policy, Brock would get notice of it. Fortunately, Turk knew the intricacies of processing claims, and with access to the American Security's systems, he could maneuver around these land mines.

Still, the possibility remained that Brock could get notice of the increase in premium and question it. Turk decided that the best way to deal with it would be to get Brock to let his homeowner's policy lapse. Turk would then pay the premium online and request the company to change the billing address to his address. He had all of Brock's personal and insurance information. It was not a crime for someone to pay the insurance premium for someone else, and the people processing the payment would never notice who made it. Turk went back to the database and learned that Brock's policy was going to expire at the end of September. The timing was perfect.

Driving to his house after work the next day, Turk heard a story on the radio about fungi, which unknown to him, were everywhere— indoors, outdoors, in food, in drywall used to construct homes—in almost infinite varieties, some good for humans and some bad. One of the bad ones was black mold. So he decided to go with that. As he drove, he concocted the scenario to weave black mold into his plan. Since time was of the essence, he decided he would try to talk to Brock first and tell him the letter was coming. As soon as he arrived at his house, he dialed Brock's phone number. Brock answered. Again, the timing was perfect.

"Mr. Brock, I don't know if you remember me, but this is Bill Malone from American Security Insurance Company."

"Yes, I do," Brock said. "You handled that fender bender where I couldn't quite get stopped and tapped the rear fender of the guy in front of me."

"Yes, that's right. Well, I've been promoted and am now in the underwriting department."

"Congratulations. You certainly did a good job handling my case. I thought that guy might try to sue and take me to the cleaners for all he could get for a bogus injury."

"Thank you," said Turk. He realized he was talking too loudly and lowered his voice. "The reason I'm calling is to let you know that you'll be receiving a letter in the next few days regarding an issue that has come up with some homes in your neighborhood regarding black mold. Since I thought receiving such a letter without any forewarning might cause some alarm or confusion, I'm calling all our insureds in your neighborhood and the surrounding areas to inform you of the situation and answer any questions you might have."

"Okay. So what is black mold?"

"Here is the situation. The plywood used for the houses built in your neighborhood was left outside in the lumberyard for months uncovered, and during this period there was a lot of rain. Because of this exposure, there is an increased risk that black mold could develop on the walls of these houses. American Security recently had a black mold claim in your neighborhood where there was a leak in the roof and the plywood got wet. The company was able to trace the problem back to that lumberyard. So American Security has decided that it will no longer insure these homes.

"None of the other insurance companies are aware of this problem or denying coverage because of it, and based on my understanding, the risk is very low that this could happen to your home. However, I would be careful not to let the inside walls of your house get wet. With your excellent claims history, you should be able to obtain homeowners insurance from any of the other major insurers."

"Okay," said Brock. "So you don't think I need to be concerned about this affecting the value of my property?"

"Technically, I can't give you formal advice on insurance or property matters, but I would say definitely not. I would not say a word about it to anyone. And I certainly would not mention it when you apply for homeowners insurance with a different company. I think if you let your policy lapse and, before that happens, you purchase your home insurance with another company, you'll be fine.

"The letter I send will tell you that you have a time limit to contest the denial of coverage, but I assume that since I've reached out to you and given you this heads-up, you'll probably just let the policy lapse and obtain insurance with another company. Is that correct?"

"Oh yes, Mr. Malone, and I do so much appreciate your contacting me. I will call another insurance company tomorrow."

"My pleasure. We value your business and hope to keep you as a client with your car insurance."

Turk drafted the declination to renew coverage letter that he would place in the mail the next morning.

By the time he had finished, it was nine in the evening. The creation of his parallel pseudofraudulent reality was now complete. As he reflected on what he had done, he realized that what he had created was much more than a mere fraud scheme. It was not a manipulation but a correction of the reality that he deserved. And while benefitting him, it was only a microscopic and imperceptible wrinkle in the vast collective consciousness. He hadn't slept much and was still being fueled by caffeine. It was time to rest and wait. The next step would be the execution of his crime.

Everything was now in place, but he knew he would have to be patient and play his cards at the appropriate times. He would submit each report a couple of days before the deadline required by the company's reporting guidelines. He would push this case through the claims process in just a few months, the time it would take Mahone to "heal," or at least heal enough that Turk would be in a position to settle the case. Smitty would be impressed by how quickly and efficiently Turk handled the claim and by his ability to settle a case with such a serious injury so cheaply.

His fictitious claim was like a seed waiting to be planted and take its rightful place coexisting side by side among the real files. Then, at the key moment—when it was time for American Security to issue the check, when it came time to deposit the real money into his bank account—Turk would cause the two parallel dimensions to overlap seamlessly.

The next morning was like any other weekday, but this one would be different. It was time for Turk to take the first step over the edge of, and perhaps into, the abyss. As soon as he called the agent and reported the claim, there would be no turning back. That phone call would set into motion the entire fabricated, fraudulent process. His life would be irrevocably changed. He would never be the same again. He would be a white-collar criminal, hopefully one who went undetected and unindicted, but an outlaw nonetheless.

Surprisingly, his conscience did not bother him like he thought it would or should. He was afraid of the consequences if he got caught, but that was it. Although his actions would be illegal and the consequences would be real, on a moral and metaphysical level, he did not feel like he would be committing an actual crime. He was doing it for a higher purpose, for a greater good, for the betterment of humankind.

Turk set his plan into motion and dialed the phone number of Brock's insurance agent, Frank Jones, the most successful and well-known insurance agent in the city. He had a huge billboard off the interstate that read, "For All Your Insurance Needs Make Just One Call. Call Frankie!"

"Good morning. American Security. Frank Jones's office." It was Frankie's assistant.

"This is John Brock. Frankie's my agent. I need to report a claim."

"I can go ahead and take the report," she responded. "What is your policy number?"

Turk had all the information ready. He gave her all the details. Mahone was a neighbor. He liked the guy. He had come over to help Turk clean out his gutters. One of the rungs on Brock's ladder broke, and Mahone had fallen and apparently broke his ankle. It looked like a pretty serious injury. Brock had driven Mahone to the emergency room, and Mahone had called his wife, who had shown up as soon as they arrived at the hospital.

Frankie's assistant explained that she would send the report to the claims office. They would assign the case to one of the claims representatives, who would contact the claimant and handle it from there. She told him not to talk about the case with anyone except the claims representative. Turk smiled. That would be easy enough.

That afternoon, he was working at his desk when the secretary from the claims processing unit entered his cubicle.

"I've got a new homeowners claim for you," she said. "It was just called in this morning. The insured is John Brock. The claimant is William Mahone. Mr. Smith said to remind you of our prompt contact policy. This looks like a pretty serious injury."

"Thank you," said Turk. "I'll jump right on it."

The file had already been set up and placed into a folder with a tab on top and a claim number. Turk opened the file and began reading the report form that contained all the same information he had given to Frankie's assistant earlier that day.

Turk opened his briefcase and pulled out the initial prompt contact with claimant form he had already prepared. He filled in the box for the contact time: September 2, 3:37 p.m. He placed the form in his outgoing tray to be collected by the staff and then date-stamped, hole punched, and inserted into the company's official file. Turk felt a smug sense of satisfaction. This was starting out even smoother than expected.

4

Oh God! The stench was unbelievable. Turk pressed the accelerator as he forced his small pickup truck up a steep incline on the makeshift road created over mountains of compacted trash. He was now deep into the county dump, climbing higher with each bend of the road. To his right was an old discarded rocking chair. On the other side, rusted bed springs burst out of the rubble. In the distance, he could see abandoned burned-out cars, used refrigerators, and an endless supply of garbage and waste as far as he could see.

Turk was wearing goggles and a facemask, but the smell was still so bad it burned his eyes. Tears streamed down his cheeks. Up until last week, he had run a weekly ad online and in the classified ads in the newspaper, offering to haul trash to the city dump for seventy-five dollars a load. Sometimes people simply had too much trash for whatever reason, remodeling their homes or whatever, that the garbage truck drivers would not take it all. There were infinite varieties of trash. Turk would haul anything. He had only one steadfast rule: he would only take cash up front before he loaded the back of the truck. He never reported the income to the IRS. It was easy, tax-free money. And Liz never knew of it, so it was not calculated into his weekly child support payments. It was just extra cash, free and clear.

But this would be his last haul, at least for the foreseeable future. He could no longer find the time. He was becoming too busy with the PPP. He had been doing research on the internet about chimpanzees. What techniques could be used to train them to perform the mundane jobs of their future owners? Where could he find chimps for purchase? How much did they cost? What would he feed them? How would he handle their excrement? He was also developing his business model and marketing plans.

After he reached the summit, he deposited his load. He moved quickly for fear of rats or other huge rodents. With his foot, he lifted a rotted piece of plywood to clear some space. Underneath, a large grayish lump of larvae oozed off the wood like a huge wad of phlegm dripping from a used tissue.

It was yet another beautiful fall day. The sky was clear. Junk and refuse extended to the horizon. Just in front of Turk was a large pool of liquid that had collected, perhaps a mixture of rainwater, oil, and discarded household chemicals. In the middle was a rusted bicycle with no wheels. The sun was just beginning to set. Its rays pierced through the clouds and smokestacks and reflected off the murky pool. The human garbage and rusted metal appeared to have coalesced into a degenerative, biological, industrial muck. Turk sensed that this place could be a seething cauldron for some new chemical reaction, possibly a new mutant life-form, something unknown, unintended, and potentially harmful. A gentle breeze picked up from the southwest, carrying a scent that was a mix of feces, burning rubber, sulfur, and rotten eggs.

As he exited, he noticed that the entrance was bordered by two huge slabs of concrete on each side. He pulled his truck to the side of the road. He always traveled with his hammer and chisel. He pulled out his tools and within a few minutes had engraved his name, Turk, into the concrete slab, where it was memorialized for posterity at the entrance to this vast wasteland. Turk was a witness.

5

It was K-day, Turk's weekend to have the kids, a Saturday morning in mid-September. He hadn't seen them in a month. He and Liz had two children: Nick, who was twelve years old, and Alicia, who was ten. Under the divorce decree, they could stay with him every other weekend, and he had visitation with them two nights a week. Something had come up—he couldn't remember what—two weeks ago when they were supposed to spend the weekend with him, so he hadn't gotten to see them. As for the weekly visitations, those had dwindled to zero.

Missing his children, not to mention Liz, even though he still carried some bitterness toward her, wasn't something Turk had foreseen happening in his life. Sometimes he felt what he thought was almost physical pain from not seeing them, an emptiness and rising anxiety emanating from deep within the pit of his stomach. He knew countless men and women experienced the same kind of pain after married life fell apart, but that didn't make it any easier.

A couple of months after the divorce decree was final, Liz had moved back to her hometown, which was two hours away, taking the kids with her. With the distance, and the added hassle factor, Turk ended up seeing them less than he could, or should. Gradually, even the number of weekend overnights had decreased.

Liz had probably known that would happen. But she had found a better job and was now close to her parents, who could help out with the kids. So how could he object? She made Nick and Alicia available when it was his turn to have them, but there was often an activity or something they were involved in that interfered. He should have hired a lawyer and filed a petition to modify the decree to maybe three weekends a month rather than two to make up for the lost visitation time during the week. But lawyers cost money, and he couldn't afford one, at least not now. He was barely able to keep up with his child support payments and the minimum payments on his credit cards. But once he succeeded in pulling off the PPP, he would be able to afford it.

Turk was not a deadbeat dad. He had never missed or even fallen behind on his child support payments. He was responsible and always met his legal obligations. He did it for the kids. And for the benefit of the kids, both he and Liz were always civil and mature in their dealings in front of them. They had to put the kids' needs above their own differences. They had been divorced for three years. During the course of the marriage, they had both changed. Liz apparently felt that they were no longer compatible and, according to her divorce petition, that the differences were irreconcilable.

Liz had been the one to initiate the breakup. All the intimate moments, the times he had opened up and confided in her, and the feelings and fears she had shared with him apparently meant nothing anymore. But they would always be parents, both of them, to their children. On the surface, it was an amicable split. They, or rather he, agreed to everything—custody, child support, visitation, and property division. Liz had a lawyer who had prepared the legal documents and the settlement agreement. When she put them in front of him, Turk hadn't even read them before he signed. He hadn't had the energy or the ability to concentrate. He couldn't even contemplate the future, much less how those documents might affect his life.

Although he understood it on an intellectual level, he just wished Liz had not moved back to her hometown. He ached to see his kids more often. And the relationship he once had with them, such as it had been since the divorce, had withered through lack of contact like a muscle that had atrophied through disuse.

Turk still felt some lingering hurt and resentment, but the anger had subsided, at least most of it. Occasionally, he would recall some random comment or accusation that would bring the painful emotions cascading back, as if he were experiencing them all over again, not as a distant memory but in the moment. She once had said that there was no more joy. Well, who was he supposed to be, *Floyd Joy*?

Liz had once told him he should get some therapy. Well, what could a therapist do for him? Could a therapist wave a magic wand and transform his boring life into something exciting? Forced to do this shit every day just so he could make a living and support his family, forced to concentrate on what American Security made him think about nearly every waking moment, as if he were blindly, contentedly sleepwalking through this endless routine—if he accepted that, he would be crazy.

And why should his mental state have been an issue at all? He had agreed to let her have custody of the kids. And her attorney had been way out of line when he referred to Turk as an odd duck. What did that mean? That wasn't a diagnosis. There was no reference to odd duckness anywhere in the DSM-5 manual of mental disorders. But once she started the legal process, things were bound to get ugly. At that point, there was no way back to what had once been. There was no way to go back home. He had no home, just a place where he lived. He had been abandoned. He had been invalidated. He was alone.

At least today he would not have to make the four-hour round trip to pick up the kids. Liz had said she was coming down for the afternoon to shop for school clothes at one of the outlet malls and that she would drop off the kids. The visitations were always awkward at first. It took time to get reacquainted. Turk had spent so much time away from his kids that he had started to idealize them in the abstract. Alicia had such a beautiful face. And Nick was such a sensitive kid. How could they ever cope with the meanness in this world and the inevitable frustrations and disappointments without Turk there to run interference?

He heard a car pulling into the driveway. It had to be Liz and the kids. He could not contain his excitement. He bolted through the front door with a huge grin on his face. But when he got to the car, there was no Nicky and no Alicia, only Liz.

"I'm so sorry," she said. "I called you a couple of times and left a voice mail."

Turk knew this part had to be true. He was continually forgetting to turn the ringer volume back up on his cell phone.

"Nick's soccer team is in the playoffs, and they made it to the finals. The game is set for tomorrow. I couldn't let him miss that game. He needs to get a good night's sleep to be ready for it. And Alicia was invited to a birthday party for one of her friends at school. It's a sleepover. You're welcome to drive up tomorrow and watch. Maybe I can make it up to you next weekend. When I couldn't reach you, I wasn't sure what to do. I hope you understand."

Turk wanted to get mad. But he actually believed her. She would not make this up. She was not vindictive in that way. He tried to think of some way to exploit the situation and use it for leverage later. But nothing came to him in the moment.

"I understand," he said. "Don't worry about it. But I think I'll have to pass on the game tomorrow. I've got too much work piled up here."

They talked about what the kids had been doing and how things were going at school. Turk maintained his composure. Rather than anger, he felt a twinge of guilt for not volunteering to drive up and watch the game the next day. She had flipped it on him again, as she had done so often when they were together. Although he normally made the drive to pick up the kids and bring them back to his place for the weekend, she was the one who had said she would make the trip this time because she had to come down anyway. She was the one who had showed up without them when it was his court-ordered time to have them. He was the one who had the right to be mad. But instead, he felt like he had done something else wrong, something else on top of all the alleged sins of the past. Even apart, he wasn't making enough effort. He was still failing to live up to her expectations.

Despite the inevitable wear-and-tear of the aging process, Liz still looked beautiful. Even though she had aged, as he had also, he did not actually see it. He could see the beginnings of wrinkles in the corners of her eyes, a slight layer of fat around her belly covered up by her sweater, and the start of a double chin. But it did not register. He saw her only through his past perception of her, the beautiful young women he had met in college. And even though, at that moment, he had the right to be angry, he didn't have the energy to muster up any more resentment.

"Say hi to the kids and tell them that I love them," said Turk, although he wasn't sure the message would get relayed. "I'll see them soon."

Turk watched Liz slowly back her car out of the driveway and into the street. As she turned her car to leave, she smiled faintly and waved. Turk responded with a slight wave and watched her drive away. Perhaps he could have, maybe should have, felt sad, but all he felt was empty.

6

By late morning that same day, the mail arrived. Turk had received a letter from the Association of International Exporters of Exotic Animals. At the top was their slogan: animals without borders—dedicated to the free trade of wild beasts.

> Thank you for your recent inquiry. Unfortunately, international trade of wild animals from Africa is illegal. However, through our contacts in the United States, we have located twelve chimpanzees for purchase. They were raised in captivity and were originally intended for shipment to a university in the United States for the purpose of AIDS research. However, because of protests by animal rights groups, the university rescinded its contract.
>
> We act solely as a broker in these transactions. Our fee is 10 percent. Any fees, miscellaneous charges, or other expenses are the responsibility of the purchaser. Because of fluctuations in the market, we cannot quote you an exact price until

the animals are ready to be shipped. It is estimated that cost will range from $10,000 to $15,000 per chimp. The quoted price will be good for seven days, and payment must be received in advance of the shipment.

If you are still interested, please send us a phone number or email address where we can reach you, and we will send you our final quote.

Turk had done enough research to know that chimpanzees were clearly the primate of choice for the PPP. Along with humans and orangutans, chimps were the only animals known to have a consciousness. They lived in small groups like humans; they had their own minisocieties. Although bonobos, which were similar to chimpanzees, were another possible candidate, they were generally considered less reliable and less hardworking. The promiscuous bonobo was a little too bohemian for Turk's purposes. He had to get chimps. But this price was outrageous.

Now that Turk was at this critical juncture with a pending offer and a potential source of funding, albeit illegal, he realized he had no clue how to go about it. He had no experience in international or domestic trade. He didn't know if he had to obtain a license to maintain these animals on his property or if it was even legal. Until this moment, he hadn't even known what it would cost to buy a chimp. He was not the *detail* guy. He was the innovator. He was the one who could step back and see things on a grander scale. He needed an assistant to deal with the details and minutiae. But obviously that wasn't an option at this point. He would have to do it all on his own.

At three o'clock the next Monday afternoon, Turk was once again cloistered in his cubicle, dictating yet another claims report. As he hunched over the file he was working on, he could feel the roll of fat around his belly. He wished he had the money to just have it instantly sucked away with a liposuction procedure. When he got dressed in the mornings, he often stood sideways and looked in the mirror. If he held his stomach in tight and simultaneously moved his head forward to stretch out the double chin, he could see the real Turk, the Turk of his youth, buried under layers of fat and aging, sagging flesh.

But Turk had a plan to deal with this. He was going to get back in shape. He was going to lose weight, exercise, and eat healthy. He had purchased a revolutionary program that he had discovered online, "Live to Eat by Eating the Living."

After he finished dictating the claims report, Turk picked up another file and began preparing for a meeting he had scheduled the next morning with one of his many claimants. Her name was Patty. This was yet another fender bender, soft-tissue injury case. Turk had already paid to have her car repaired. She had gone to the emergency room and complained of some minor neck pain.

When he was done reviewing the file, he looked up and, in that moment of broader awareness, realized he was bored to the point of almost complete immobilization. He stared at the picture of Nick and Alicia he kept on his desk. He remembered when Nick was born; it had seemed like the world was full of endless possibilities. It was a perfect moment, an extraordinary moment. The banal reality, the hard work, the sleepless nights, the arguments—all that came later. That instant in time was complete within itself, inextricably bound with the future and Nick's unlimited potential. Nick was perfect in that present moment, and anything was possible.

After Alicia was born, it seemed ideal, a boy and a girl. But ultimately, the years of adjusting claims and the daily work routine had sucked the passion for life out of Turk's being. As he drafted reports and shuffled documents, he felt like his senses had gradually dulled and his mind had become progressively, chronically numb. There were so many details to worry about. He was mired in minutiae. He could no longer discern what was important and what was trivial and whether any of it really mattered. The time spent in this monotonous realm of his existence far exceeded the moments in which he felt truly alive.

He had several denial letters he needed to prepare. He hated doing these. With denial letters, he had to write the claimant and tell the person that he had investigated his or her claim but did not think his insured was at fault. Thus, American Security was not liable and would not pay. These cases had piled up because he kept putting them off. He hated saying no to people. He much preferred to seek others' approval.

He had a form letter he had created for denials. All he had to do was change the names, date of loss, and the claim number. He had sent this letter to countless claimants, making subtle little changes along the way. He felt it had slowly evolved into a work of art. The goal of the letter was to appear to be saying something while actually saying nothing, to appear to be clear while actually being intentionally vague.

He pulled up the document onto his computer screen.

Dear _____:

Thank you for allowing us the opportunity to investigate your claim. At American Security, we pride ourselves on our proactive, knowledge-driven, and fair-minded approach as we use industry best-practices in processing claims and continually strive to provide the best claim service in the country.

After a thorough investigation, it has been determined that our insured was not at fault and American Security has no legal obligation in regard to this incident. American Security therefore declines to make a payment at this time ...

Turk always used the passive voice; it was easier to dodge responsibility. It hadn't been his decision. This had been decreed by some anonymous group of wise people. And he never got specific. With ambiguity came a lack of accountability.

Our decision was based on a plethora of reasons …

Turk never went on to state what those reasons were. Turk had inserted the word *plethora* into his form letter just for the hell of it. It was another word for *many* but was obscure enough that many people would not know what it meant. This would throw them off just as they were getting the bad news. More importantly, it sounded to Turk like the name of a female sexual organ. He couldn't resist sticking it into the hundreds of these letters that he was forced to write. In some insignificant way, he was rebelling, raging against the fact that in order to make a living, he was forced to think about this shit all day, every day.

As Felix had sung in the lyrics to one of his last songs, "Descartes wrote, 'I think, therefore, I am.' Well man, I am forced to think boring thoughts; therefore, I am bored. You can try to control my mind, but you'll never steal my soul."

Turk never put his name on the letter. No need for him to put himself out there. Better to stay anonymous. It simply ended,

Sincerely,
Claims Department

He knew he had responsibilities and that there were lot of jobs out there that were much worse and paid a lot less, but his job consumed his conscious, waking life with American Security's agenda. Unlike a factory job or driving a truck, he couldn't just put one part of his brain on automatic pilot to accomplish a certain task and let the rest of his mind wander into the nether regions. These activities required some concentration and therefore his attention and, he believed, the use of a greater portion of his brain.

For the time that his superiors consumed his awareness of life with these mundane tasks, he was sucked into their reality and under their influence. They were exercising mind control. He was forced to think about what they wanted him to think. He was forced to use their forms, their system, their methods, and their calculations. Even though he didn't really buy into any of it, this was how he made a living. So he had no choice but to start thinking like them. He thought he could feel subtle changes in his brain. Maybe they were chemical, electrical, or even physical changes to his gray matter or whatever. He didn't know. But his bosses were framing his view of reality. He realized that he had changed, that they had changed him, and that they may have altered the physical structure of his brain and, therefore, his entire being. Turk didn't think it was possible that he could ever get back to where or who he had once been.

Every time he tried to disengage his mind from the job, he experienced withdrawal. He would ruminate on meaningless, insignificant details: things he might have forgotten to do, deadlines he might have missed, inappropriate comments he might have made, subtle slights by others. Had anyone noticed the brief moment where he lacked discretion and checked out the mailroom clerk's butt? Sometimes he would be consumed by these thoughts for the entire drive home from work. If he did not force himself to think about something else, his mind would fall into the default mode that had apparently been hardwired into his brain. He couldn't help it.

And if that wasn't enough, he was supposed to be grateful to his superiors and to American Security, thankful to have a job, content to have found his secure niche in the vast economic system. So perhaps this was his life and all that it might ever be, though much less than he once dreamed it would be. And if so, if he were forced to play along, he could at least take a few meaningless, undetectable, anonymous jabs for freedom of thought.

But ultimately, the unhappiness and frustration, the emotional pain, did serve one useful purpose: it confirmed his existence. It reminded him that he was alive, like pinching himself to make sure it was real and not a dream. The monotony of his existence could have dulled him into submission, but the pain forced him to realize with each passing moment that he did, in fact, exist.

Maybe he had sunk to the level where he was like a drug addict or an alcoholic in the throes of an addiction, clinging to the substance despite the pain as a link to something exciting, connected, and joyful in the past. Perhaps as he aged, he was trying to cling to a part of himself or what he once thought was his self-identity, a faint youthful image formed in a different place and time. And with each attempt to reignite his worn-out neural pathways, he sensed only a faint recollection of the exhilaration he had once felt when he was young. But he knew that he was awake. He was still conscious. He was alive!

7

They came to his house and installed the water softener while he was at work. He had left the key under the doormat. The softener company had offered a special plan with no payment up front. If he paid the bill within six months, he would not have to pay any interest. He didn't have the money to pay for it right then, so he would simply use one of his credit cards. If this caused his debt to increase too much, he would do what he had done many times before and take advantage of one of the numerous credit card offers he received almost daily. He would pay the bill with one of his existing cards and then transfer the balance on that card to a new card offering zero percent interest for six months on all balance transfers.

With the new softener, he would never again have to deal with scaly deposits in his bathroom or rings in his toilets. This winter, he would be free from dry skin. He had never really thought about it, but when he read their ad in the Sunday newspaper, he realized that this company could take care of a problem that he had never realized he had. In marketing his PPP, he could learn from them.

This company was truly remarkable. They had not just found a need. They had created a need, filled it, and found a way to make a profit from it. They had taken something from nature and improved upon it. In the process, they had changed the language used to describe it, and in so doing, they changed the very nature in which people perceived it.

They had created *soft* water. Unlike *hard* water, it wasn't just a resource anymore. It was a product.

8

A couple of weeks passed, each day like the day before or the day after. Finally, one evening after dinner, Turk logged onto his computer and his life changed. He clicked on an unread email, and a document loaded onto his screen.

> Republique Togolaise
> Nigerian National Petrochemical Consortium
> Strictly Confidential
>
> From the desk of: Dr. Abubakar Okaro, BSC, MSC, PhD
> Re: Transfer of $27.5 Million into Offshore Account
>
> Dear Mr. Malone:
>
> Through confidential inquiries made through your country's chamber of commerce, we have chosen you and a few other carefully selected individuals to contact regarding this opportunity. We would like to solicit your assistance with this mutually

beneficial transaction to which we hope you will give your urgent attention.

I served as chairman of the National Government Contract Review Panel under the regime of General Abdulsalami Abubakar and with the assistance of my four panel members was able to set aside $27.5 million, which we discovered were misappropriated funds from grossly overbilled contracts.

My colleagues and I are all planning to leave this country and immigrate to the United States, but before we can do this, we need to get this money out of the country and into a secure account in the US.

If you agree to help us, you will be well-compensated for your assistance. All you need to do is allow us to transfer the funds from our Nigerian bank account into your back account in the US. For simply being a recipient of this money, you will receive a generous commission of 20 percent of the total funds transferred, which is $5.5 million. My colleagues and I will take the other 80 percent and from that amount pay off any expenses.

With the money being transferred to your account, you will be taking no risk of being omitted from this transaction. In fact, it is we who are taking the risk, which is why we have so thoroughly checked out your background before contacting you with this opportunity.

Could you please notify me immediately of your acceptance to carry out this transaction at my email address listed below? Because of my country's poor communication system, you might have to try several times to get through to me. I shall inform you of the modalities for a formal application to secure the necessary approvals for immediate release of these funds into your account.

Respectfully,
Dr. Abubakar Okaro, BSC, MSC, PhD

Turk knew all about the Nigerian scam. The trick was to use the lure of easy money to entice the victim into giving out his or her checking account number, tapping into the victim's own greed. Then, instead of transferring millions of dollars, the Nigerians would withdraw any money that was in the account and transfer it to their own offshore bank account. Hapless victims would wake up not to riches but to a zero balance in their bank accounts. They would feel cheated, victimized, devastated, duped, stupid, but also guilty for participating in what was, in hindsight, such an obvious scheme.

But Turk was wise to these guys. And this fortuitous inquiry had presented itself at the perfect time. Turk knew that on his own he was incapable of sifting through the morass of red tape and legal requirements involved in trying to purchase the chimps legitimately. And he didn't have the funds to enlist anyone's help with this enterprise. His best option, therefore, was to go underground and search for his chimps on the black market. The process was already set in motion. He had already created the fictitious claim that would take him outside the law. And engaging in illegal activity was all these guys did. They certainly had all sorts of nefarious contacts. What's more, they were in Africa. Who better to approach about buying chimps underground? Turk clicked the Reply tab at the top of the screen and typed in his response.

Dear Dr. Okaro:

I read with enthusiasm your proposal regarding the transfer of funds from your country to my bank account. Although I am not able to participate in such a transaction at this time, I do have an opportunity I would like to discuss with you and which I believe would be extremely lucrative and mutually beneficial. I can only discuss this with you by telephone or in person. Please provide me with a phone number where I can reach you and a time that you would be available. I await your reply.

Sincerely,
William Malone

Turk clicked Send. Like he always did, he clicked on it three times just to make sure it went through, and as he did, he felt a sense of empowerment. He was operating at a higher level now. He was transcending.

Turk awoke in the middle of the night to a loud clap of thunder. Intense rain and hail pounded on his roof. Out the back window, flashes of lightning spread across the horizon, igniting and illuminating the entire sky. He was in the epicenter of a vast storm. The wind had shifted so that it was now blowing from north to south, sweeping across the waste treatment plant. The smell of human excrement mixed with chemicals overwhelmed him. He got out of bed and turned on the air-conditioner, hoping it would help filter out some of the stench. He rushed to the garage, where he had a box of masks that fit over his nose and mouth. Despite these measures, the caustic fumes invaded the entire house. Turk felt them seeping into the pores of his skin and irritating the whites of his eyes.

He lay down on the floor next to his portable air-purifying system and switched it on. He removed the mask, and the sterilized air blew forcefully into his face and up his nostrils. Still, he could not escape the smell. But this was manageable. And he took some comfort knowing that his own feces was part of the collective waste that made up this awful odor.

As the storm continued, he started to get groggy, but each time he was on the verge of falling back to sleep, another shock wave of thunder woke him, followed by a flash of lightning. He lay on his side, the purified air shooting full into his face, and lingered in a twilight state of consciousness. He drifted into a distant memory. It came in spurts like a long-distance phone call with a bad connection, broken up by static or periods of silence. Some parts were not intact or recoverable. Other parts were clear and distinct. He may have revised some of them and embellished other parts. He did not know.

It was the spring of my junior year in college. As I left class, I noticed a flyer that advertised summer jobs. Since I had not prepared well, I had nothing lined up for the summer. The flyer advertised a "sales opportunity" that would give me the chance to make a lot of money in a short time, meet interesting people, and develop marketable skills for the future. "See our booth at the student job fair."

I couldn't resist looking into the opportunity. I needed to start exploring all possibilities. I had a C+ grade point average. So basically, life as I knew it was over. I was only twenty-one, not yet even out of college, but the die was cast. My options were already dwindling. There would be no medical school, no law school, no MBA. I would never be able to get into any decent graduate school with my grades. The only way it could happen now was if I could score high on the entrance exams and make straight As my senior year. There was no other way to make up the deficit. I was already behind and trying to make up the difference. I was already sinking.

It wasn't as if I hadn't tried. I thought I was making the right moves but must have been on the wrong grid. Somehow things didn't connect up. It was as if I had taken a class where attendance was not required and there was only a final exam. Then two weeks before the end of the term, I suddenly realized I had forgotten to attend the class. Now I was so far behind I could never catch up.

I entered the job fair and went directly to a booth that had a huge banner advertising Encyclopedia Kidacornicopia. Below, it read, *A door to the infinite world of knowledge, written especially for kids, in language they can understand and geared to their unique interests and point of view. Parents can contribute to their child's development with this gift of a lifetime. Right now.*

I was hooked. Here was an opportunity to make big money and at the same time provide others with a product that could improve their lives. This was perfect. They had found a need that I never knew existed and developed this encyclopedia to fill that need. I signed on for the adventure.

I spent the summer with the other student-salespersons, exploring the vast areas of suburban sprawl throughout the Midwest. We all traveled together in an old bus that had been converted into a mobile minidormitory. Some of the seats had been ripped out and replaced with sleeping bunks.

We filed out of the bus every morning and saturated the "target area," going door-to-door, cold-calling, trying to sell our kiddy encyclopedias. After a hard day on the streets of suburbia, we would get together and share stories. I related my experiences chatting up overweight women in sheer see-through nightgowns and women in their thirties or forties who had slight, sometimes obvious, pockets of fat packed around their hips and stomachs, the type of padding that comes with bearing children. Some would come to the door with curlers in their hair. The television was always on with a soap opera playing in the background. Their husbands were at work.

Some were still sexy. As they talked and the sun shined through their sheer gowns, revealing bulky inner thighs, sometimes I wondered if perhaps they were open to a quick encounter as a way to escape their mundane daily routines.

Somehow at that age, still young and thin, I had managed to charm many of these middle-aged women and convince them to buy the book. I talked to them about the need to do whatever it took to ensure their kids' futures, give them an edge, a leg up. I thought I could see through the layers of cellulite and the years of drudgery and rediscover, buried deep, what were still beautiful faces and what they still saw sometimes when they looked in the mirror. Somehow I managed to sell lots of kiddy encyclopedias and make a lot of money as viewed within that market, that paradigm. This gave me a high status among the others in the group.

Some of the lower producers occasionally came to me for advice. How did I do it? That was when I got tagged with the nickname Turk. I replied on several occasions, "Just chat them up, be a little flirtatious, act like you are interested in their boring lives. Don't be afraid to make a fool of yourself. Don't be afraid to be a 'turkey.'"

And late one night, on one of the bunks in the back row of the bus, there was magic. I had become friends with one of the coeds. For some reason, she lay down next to me. Everyone else was asleep. I pulled a blanket over us as we nestled onto the narrow bunk— the best we could do under the circumstances. She was slender, sexy, and beautiful, though her looks were not so stunning that she was intimidating. She was just ordinary enough that she was approachable. I knew better than to overreach. The average and the elite, the ordinary and the beautiful, did not coalesce smoothly into the human gene pool.

I asked if I needed to use protection. She said she had it covered. Her thighs were soft, her hips rhythmic. That was the first of many such encounters.

Sometimes me and my sales buddies would smoke dope and get high early in the morning before starting our door-to-door cold calls. Rather than split up and canvass the neighborhoods separately as we usually did and had been instructed to do, we hit the streets together, a pack of roving entrepreneurs, laughing at the absurdity of the world.

For that brief period, my life was an overwhelming dopamine rush, as if someone had taken a microscopic needle and injected the neurotransmitter into the prefrontal cortex of my brain. I couldn't get enough sex. I couldn't party enough. I couldn't drink enough. I couldn't smoke enough dope. I couldn't get high enough. There was no time or need for sleep. I was pushing boundaries. I kept pushing those kiddy encyclopedias during the day and pushing the pleasure button every night. I could break the mold after all. I could be the first Dionysiac salesman!

9

Despite the rough night, Turk was at work promptly at 8:30 the next morning. It was September 30, exactly twenty-eight days since he had submitted his initial prompt contact with claimant form for Mr. Mahone. The interim basic report was due within thirty days. He had already prepared it and was waiting for the appropriate amount of time to pass. He placed it in his out basket two days ahead of schedule—excellent compliance with the reporting deadlines.

Now he had to wait for Mr. Mahone to recover. Turk had inflicted poor Mahone with an injury that took at least three months to heal. And until it healed, he could not settle the case. But only a serious injury would generate the amount of money he needed. Three to four months was a little quick to get the claim settled but within the range of plausibility

Turk had already prepared all the required reports. The next step was the interim status report. He would submit that on October 28. In that report, he had already summarized the claimant's status at that time and attached copies of additional pertinent medical records and the updated doctors' reports. He would submit the liability/settlement evaluation report on November 26 and hope he could get approval to settle the claim in December.

That afternoon, he drove to the apartment of one of his claimants, Patty. He had previously scheduled the appointment with her to try to settle her auto claim. She lived alone and rented half of a double on the northeast side of town. Unlike most rentals, this house was not divided into two sides but rather a front and a back. To get to her unit, Turk had to enter through a gate into the fenced-in backyard. He closed the latch and turned toward the back door.

In that instant, he heard a loud bark and in his peripheral vision could see a huge dog running toward him. He turned to face the beast as it closed in. It was a Doberman pinscher. Turk froze. He was experiencing one of his worst primal fears. An electric jolt seared from the base of his skull downward throughout his entire body as if he had just received a deathblow to the brain stem. His penis and testicles retracted. There was no time to get the pepper spray he always carried in his briefcase. The sleek creature was upon him with its jaws wide open, baring its sharp, glimmering teeth. It lunged toward his throat.

He could see it all in that moment. He had handled countless dog-bite claims. If he was lucky, he might escape with a huge gaping wound on his leg or ripped flesh sagging off his forearm. Blood would spurt everywhere and ooze into the fabric of his clothes. He would need stitches. Hopefully his face would be spared; otherwise, they would have to summon a plastic surgeon to the emergency room. He would insist on that, even if doped up or on morphine. The wounds might get infected. He would incur huge medical bills. He would miss work. If he wasn't so lucky, the animal would maul him. His entire body would be torn apart. He might not survive the attack.

He pulled his briefcase up in front of his face like a shield. He could see only the dog's hind legs as it sprung toward him, suspended in midair. He braced for the impact. But there was none. Instead, he heard a loud high-pitched guttural screech. He lowered the briefcase. The canine's forward thrust had stopped abruptly. Its hind legs continued forward, but its upper body fell backward and slammed to

the ground. The animal was restrained by a collar that was attached
to a long chain. The beast quickly jumped back to its feet and lunged
again. The chain made a snapping sound as it fully extended. The
collar tightened around the dog's throat, and it fell backward again.
It kept barking. Turk focused on the stake to which the chain was
attached, hoping it would not give way as the animal kept pulling
against it, trying to get to him.

His entire body went limp as he realized that he had been spared
this time. His knees started to buckle, but he steadied himself. As
the numbness wore off, he could feel his penis start to enlarge as the
blood began flowing again.

Patty poked her head outside the back door.

"Don't mind him," she said. "He belongs to the people who live
in front. They keep him as a watchdog. Thank God they keep him
chained. I told them they also need to put a sign on the fence. But
they don't listen to me. I hope he didn't scare you. I'm sorry. I should
have told you to watch out for him."

"That's okay," responded Turk. "No harm, no foul."

They sat down at Patty's kitchen table. Turk opened his briefcase
and pulled out the release and settlement agreement and his official
American Security checkbook. He had the authority to write checks
up to $10,000 without obtaining prior approval from his superiors.

"Let's see," said Turk. "We've already had your car repaired.
It looks like we paid almost $1,500 for that. And you incurred, it
looks like, about $750 in bills from the emergency room, which
includes the charges for the x-rays, the hospital and the emergency
room doctor …"

Patty nodded in agreement. This was the crucial moment
in obtaining a truly excellent settlement on this type of case. By
this point, a number of people would have talked with a lawyer
or a cousin or someone who would have told them about the huge
settlement their friend had received after an accident. Those cases
could not be settled cheaply. But there were also a number of people
out there who were unsophisticated in these matters and didn't know

anything about things like compensation for pain and suffering or lost wages. So Turk never brought up any of that stuff. It wasn't his job to educate them. It was all just legalese anyway. He'd offer to pay her medical bills in a matter-of-fact manner, as if this was how these matters were always handled, and see she if took the bait. If not, he could always increase his settlement offer.

"So if you'll just sign here," Turk continued, "I'll go ahead and make out the check to you in the amount of $750."

"Oh, thank you," she said. She seemed genuinely appreciative. She picked up the pen.

Turk started to feel a twinge of guilt. "You might want to read the release first."

"Oh, sure. You're right. I guess I should. But I don't really understand these things. I think I'll grab a bottled water. Would you like one? I'm sorry. I should have offered it when you first sat down."

"Sure, if you're having one."

She stood up from the table and opened the refrigerator door.

"Oh, I'm sorry," he blurted out. "Did I say $750? That encounter with the dog must have distracted me. I forgot to include anything for your *inconvenience* ..." He never used the phrase "pain and suffering."

She sat back down at the table and set down the two bottles of water. Turk pulled out a new release form.

"Here. Let's redo this. Did I say $750? Let's add another $100 just to make up for all the hassle you had to deal with. So that will come to $850. No. Let's make it an extra $200. What the hell. We'll make it $250. That way we'll end up with an even $1,000. How does that sound?"

"That would be wonderful. Thank you so much. That is so nice of you."

"You're very welcome," said Turk. "Just sign and date the release at the bottom, and I'll cut the check."

A thousand dollars was well within the settlement range at which he had evaluated the case in his report, so there would be no negative repercussions. When he left, he had to walk through the backyard once again. This time Patty stood on the back porch, and the dog did not move. Once Turk had exited through the gate and was standing safely outside the fence, he turned around, stared the animal directly in the eyes, and grinned. He got no reaction. The beast seemed completely indifferent to him.

As Turk drove back to the office, he reflected on his encounter with that domesticated but wild beast. He had nearly suffered a serious injury, something real and painful. In his job, he spent countless numbing hours evaluating other people's supposed pain and suffering. But what he almost experienced had not been an abstract calculation. It had almost happened to him. He experienced so much of his life vicariously. When he watched the news on television, he was a detached observer. In his internet travels, he was anonymous, unknown, and safe. He did not actually experience so much of the life that he lived.

When Turk arrived at the office the next morning, he went straight to the men's restroom. When he had finished washing and drying his hands, he placed the moist paper towel in the palm of his left hand. This would allow him to use the paper towel to open the door without having to touch the handle. He would then have two options. If someone else was in the restroom, Turk would time his actions so that this sucker would grab the handle and open the door and Turk would exit right behind him. Turk would wad up the wet towel, put it in his pocket, and later discard it in the wastebasket at his desk.

If there was no one around, he would use the paper towel to grab the handle, open the door wide enough to prop it open with his left foot, spin to his right, take a long step forward with his right leg, and then stretch his left arm over to the trash container mounted on the wall. He would then release the wet wad into the bin and exit the restroom.

This elaborate ritual was necessary because the idiot who designed the building had made the door to the restroom open toward the inside. To enter, one could simply push open the door. But that was when it didn't matter. Everyone knew that a lot of men were lazy and did not wash their hands after taking a piss. Worse, there were tons of self-centered assholes out there who had no qualms about taking a shit, wiping their big, fat, hairy butts, and then nonchalantly exiting the stall and heading straight for the door without going near the sink.

This all meant that the greatest risk Turk faced every day, the most likely source for contracting an illness from countless germs and diseases, was that tainted door handle that he was forced to grasp—because of the incompetence of the designer—in order to get out of the restroom. It didn't matter that Turk washed his hands before touching it unless everyone else did. Who would ever design a public restroom under the assumption that everyone would follow the rules of proper public hygiene? Only an incompetent architect or builder would assume that one could construct anything in this world without accounting for the inherent incompetence and self-centeredness of the majority of the people who inhabited it.

As Turk passed through the lobby into the main office, he smiled and nodded politely to the receptionist. She did not respond. She never actually looked at him. She appeared to be in her early forties and was probably divorced and raising a kid or two on her own. There was no question that, out of everyone in the office, she was absolutely the lowest person in the hierarchy. Someone had to be last. It was clear that she didn't like it. And who could blame her? Turk felt sorry for her but knew it was best to keep his distance.

She had set up strict boundaries like a cat staking out its territory by pissing around the perimeter. Turk could almost smell the scent of dried urine. She arrived every morning at exactly 8:30, took lunch precisely from 12:30 to 1:15, put the phones on voice mail at 4:45 p.m., and left.

Turk decided that he would try to engage her in a casual conversation. She seemed so isolated and sad.

"So how are you doing this morning?" he asked.

"Fine," she responded. But as she said it, she stiffened. She didn't look up at him and uttered her response in a monotone that he could barely hear. The passive aggression was palpable. It emanated from her like a strong body odor, one that couldn't be covered up with deodorant or antiperspirant.

When Turk arrived at his desk, a memo from Smitty lay on top of his pile of mail.

> To: Turk Malone, Senior Claims Representative
> From: Allen S. Smith, Executive Vice President and
> Regional Claims Manager
> Re: Insured: Brock
>
> Claim No.: AS-1-S3-HO-666-LE
> Good job in complying with our prompt contact policy. Press ahead for the medical records, especially Dr. Simpson's. Keep up the good rapport with the claimant.

This was great. Smitty had taken the bait and was treating this fictitious claim like a real one. But was this oversight what he had to look forward to with Smitty as his new boss? Would he monitor and micromanage Turk's files and send inane memos advising him to do what he was going to do anyway? Was Smitty really just sending a reminder to him that he was being watched?

Whatever. Now Turk was in control, and his embezzlement scheme that would ultimately enable him to actualize his PPP was going as planned.

It looked like this might be even easier than he had thought. And the additional bonus would be making a fool out of ol' Smitty. He was, after all, everything Turk despised and feared. It was not just that he was too much the fresh face and had probably been an Eagle Scout or a top athlete or the president of his senior class in high school. Although now that Turk had kids, who he unfortunately saw less and less, he had gotten over his past frustrations and had high hopes for his children as Liz put them through a regimen similar to the one he had experienced as a child. He wanted those same kinds of achievements for his kids. He wanted them to make good grades and get into a top college. He wanted them to be popular. He wanted them to have high self-esteem and feel good about themselves.

But what frightened him about Smitty was the idea that there had to be some type of underlying mindset that would result in the smug, arrogant expression that was always on his face. It was a mindset that could attach to greed, ideologies, dogmas, movements—whatever—combined with a lack of empathy or sensitivity or maybe just a lack of compassion. Perhaps Smitty was a concrete thinker, incapable of abstract thought. Turk didn't know. Smitty seemed absolutely certain of his actions, no second-guessing, no cognitive dissonance, no matter how misguided or incompetent. He was aggressively stupid.

One could take that smug demeanor, transport him back through a time warp, and place him in the Third Reich, and he would fit right in: *Smitty—psycho Nazi man.* Maybe Turk just resented him because he was his boss. But Turk was sure of one thing: he had figured this guy out. Smitty was evil!

10

That night, like so many others, he could not fall asleep. He got out of bed, and it was two o'clock in the morning. He sat down at his desk and stared into his computer screen. He had to work up to this moment like a bulimic binge-eating but dreading the upcoming purge. He could not resist the taste, but he knew the pain would come. He would feel the eruption of contents from his stomach, the momentary ballooning of his esophagus, and then the peaceful feeling of an empty stomach again.

He typed in the word *viatical*. This was truly a predator's market, potentially lucrative but risky. He had never engaged in one of these transactions. He didn't have the money to invest. This was research into another venture that he might pursue if the PPP didn't work out. The standard viatical deal involved a person who was terminally ill and needed money to pay for medical bills and other expenses that came along with a death sentence decreed by the laws of nature. They had life insurance policies, but those only paid out at the time of death. These dying people needed money now. When they bought the policy years ago, leaving money to their family and loved ones, they had been contemplating a quicker, more "natural" death. Now, in pain, in debt, and in need, they realized the financial instrument they had purchased and paid premiums on throughout their entire healthy life did not address their present needs. They wanted to live.

They wanted to get their hands on that pent-up cash now so they could use it to pay for some kind of treatment, something that could help them hang on just a little longer, until there was a cure, until the Second Coming, until someone had finally discovered the fountain of youth, or whatever. With such a universal need, there was an endless market, however sad it might be.

Turk had checked out this site a couple of times previously. And just like tonight, he had felt dirty. But like trees decaying in the forest, life fed off death. It was all part of the same grand scheme of life and death and regeneration. By making money off it, he would be no worse than any parasite in nature. Unlike funeral directors, cemetery owners, and probate attorneys who made money off death, this transaction offered hope. It was truly a financial instrument that found a need and then filled that need.

In the typical deal, the person who was terminally ill, the client, would sell his or her life insurance policy for an amount far less than its face value. The investor would pay that amount in one lump sum to the client and also agree to pay the future premiums. In exchange, the client would change the beneficiary to the investor. The terminally ill client could then use that money to pay for needed health care. When the policy matured—that is, when the client died—the investor would receive the insurance proceeds. The way to make money on these deals was to find people whose conditions were so serious that they would likely die in the very near future. If the investor picked someone who might linger on, the investor would lose money and get stuck paying the premiums until the client died. Accordingly, Turk knew that if he ever got into this market, he would have to focus on only the most virulent diseases and deadliest forms of cancer.

The information from the website loaded onto his screen. After a brief search, he found a lead that looked promising. The potential client was a poor man in his late fifties with colorectal cancer, Duke's stage C, poorly differentiated. He had a life insurance policy worth half a million dollars with his wife named as the beneficiary. The tumor had already invaded the surrounding lymph nodes, but there was no evidence of metastasis, where the cancer cells break off into the blood stream and spread to other parts of the body. So there was potential here, but this case was borderline. Once the cancer had invaded the lymph nodes, it was quite possible that the metastasis had already occurred but was not yet detectable.

Even if they eradicated the cancer at the site, it could already have seeded into the lungs, the brain, or the liver—anywhere. The survival rate at this advanced stage was very poor. If there was evidence of metastasis, this case would be a slam dunk, but without that, it could be a risky investment. If the client somehow beat the odds or lingered on, the investor would be stuck paying the premiums for a very long time. And a case like this would take a lot of work. If Turk decided to go ahead, he'd have to go through the process of reducing this *guy* to an abstraction—a client. He would have to focus solely on the transaction and ignore the tragedy of this person's disease. Even if he did have the money, he knew he wouldn't be able to do it. He was not capable of making a profit off someone else's suffering. Besides, with so much to be done on his PPP, and now a fraud in progress, there wasn't enough time to pursue this opportunity.

He went back to his bedroom but still wasn't tired. He had learned from many years of experience that it did him no good to try to fall asleep in this state of arousal. All he did was lie awake and ruminate. To help put him into a drowsy state, he kept a stack of reading materials next to his bed. He always needed to do more background reading on his most important project, the PPP, the one that would make him rich and change the world, the one that had truly found one of the most fundamental of all needs—the need to be free from the drudgery of work—and filled it. He had printed numerous articles about chimpanzees and other primates from the internet. He had taken out several books from the public library, which were now overdue.

As he learned more about chimps, he realized the possibilities went far beyond just freedom from the mind-numbing boredom of everyday life and the constant need to pay attention to endless details. The forging of a mind-body meld between raw animal power and technological, computerized intelligence would likely result in the creation of a new type of primate: a techno-monkey, a super yet subordinate chimp. They could be bred and trained. This could be the beginning of a vast new underclass. They could be the source of an endless supply of cheap labor. They could be exploited for vast profits. They could be sent to war. The potential was limitless.

He opened a thick book from his stack of reading materials, titled *The Bible of Baboon Behavior: A Primer on Primates*. He knew the key was to understand. Knowledge was power. Once he understood, then he could manipulate and control. If he wasn't the strongest chimp, he had to be the smartest, unless he just wanted to go with the flow. And that was okay for some people. He realized he needed these types of people. In fact, he needed a lot of them. Otherwise, to whom would he sell? Who could he lead? Who would there be to push around?

He opened the thick treatise to a page he had marked about halfway through the book.

> In order to understand baboons, you need to have a broader, general view of the behavior of all primates, an evolutionary group of which humans are a part. We've all heard the slang term "top dog," but how few of us have ever stopped to consider its significance when applied to our own lives, as primates, as human beings, which also means that part of our "humanness" is the primate or animal part of our being?

The fundamental concept is dominance. A hierarchy exits in nature in every wolf pack, dog pack, and group of chimpanzees. Is it therefore any surprise that these same hierarchies and power structures would exist in the mind of the ultimate primate—the human being? Look at all the weapons humans have created, from bows and arrows to guns to weapons of mass destruction for the purpose of protecting themselves and dominating others. These two forces are inextricably linked—fear and dominance. The human response to the fear of being killed is to kill. All primates want to live, to survive. We humans use our refined intellects to satisfy our most basic primate needs. So we must not fool ourselves. The need to dominate, the hierarchy, is still ingrained in our species. Take, for example, office politics …

Turk flipped to the section on chimpanzees. There was a picture of Washoe, the first chimpanzee ever trained to use sign language. The first chapter dealt with the horrors inflicted on chimps used for medical research. They had been through hell, infected with HIV, all sorts of awful things. Many had suffered self-inflicted wounds. One chewed off his finger. It was common practice among many lab chimps to smear and even eat their own feces.

Turk put down the book and picked up from the top of the stack an article he had downloaded off the internet. It was about a disabled Nigerian boy who had been adopted and raised by chimpanzees for eighteen months. His name was Bello. He was found with a family of chimps deep in the forest. He had a deformed forehead and had probably been abandoned by his human parents.

Finally, Turk began to get drowsy. His head slumped back against the pillow he had propped up behind his back, and he lapsed into unconsciousness.

11

When Turk arrived home after work the next day, he immediately logged onto his computer. The email he was waiting for had arrived. He clicked on Unread Mail, and the message loaded onto the screen.

> Republique Togolaise
> Nigerian National Petrochemical Consortium
> **Strictly Confidential**
> From the desk of: Dr. Abubakar Okaro, BSC, MSC, PhD
> Re: Transfer of $27.5 Million into Offshore Account
>
> Dear Mr. Malone:
> I am responding to your email regarding an opportunity which you think would be lucrative and mutually beneficial. Although we find this request highly unusual, I am willing to have my associate Mr. Jaleel Abdullah contact you to discuss this opportunity. Please provide me with your phone

number, and I will have him call you tomorrow at 8:00 p.m. EST.

Respectfully,
Dr. Abubakar Okaro

Turk immediately clicked the Reply tab at the top of the screen, typed in his phone number, and responded that he would eagerly await the phone call from Mr. Abdullah.

The next morning at work, Turk logged onto his computer, and there was a message tagged with a red exclamation point. It was from Stan Crane, his immediate supervisor, who reported directly to Smitty.

> To: Turk Malone
> From: Stan Crane
> Re: Insured: Spendel
>
> Claim no.: 52-A-903-SS
> In your interim report submitted three months ago, you said that you would be following up to obtain the remaining medical bills and would then be ready to settle the case. I have received nothing since that time. And your settlement evaluation report is overdue. Have you done anything on this case in the last several months? Please promptly advise so that we can stay in compliance with the company's reporting guidelines.
>
> Cc: A. Smith, Regional Claims Manager
> Master File

Smitty must have gotten to him. Turk had always known Crane was dangerous, a kiss ass, pliable, a potential Nazi sympathizer.

Subject to the influence of someone like Smitty, a guy like Crane could be manipulated into doing almost anything. He would turn on a coworker in an instant. Turk had known Crane for years. He could easily have strolled across the office and talked to him face-to-face. He could have sent a short email only to Turk asking for a status update. By sending this type of terse, abrupt email and copying Smitty, Crane was clearly stabbing Turk in the back and trying to score points with Smitty. It was obvious that Smitty's game of divide and conquer had already started, and his first recruit was the biggest dumbass in the office.

Well, if Crane wanted to play it that way, if he wanted to hang ol' Turk out to dry, then Turk would respond in kind. Crane had started it. He was the one who had pushed the nuclear button. So now Turk needed only to worry about saving himself. He knew how to create revisionist documentation, revisionist history, and revisionist reality, and he would use those abilities to make sure he didn't look bad to Smitty. Instead, he would make Crane look bad. He would show no mercy.

He reached down and opened the bottom drawer of his desk. Using both hands, he lifted up a huge binder and dropped it on top: *A Compendium of the Writings of Felix.* Turk had printed off a copy from his home computer and kept it at his office.

Turk opened it to the section titled "Ode to the Amygdala—the Seat of Unbridled Terror." This was the part of the brain where fear originated. He continued reading into the next chapter, "Ride Those Raging Hormones." Once he finished, he felt better. Part of Felix's philosophy dealt with the ongoing human struggle to reconcile the functioning of different parts of the brain that had evolved over time. Felix occasionally ended his grandiose discourses with practical tidbits of advice. In this instance, Felix advised that Turk had no control over what Crane had done. But he could control his reaction to it. Felix, no doubt, was referring to a more civilized, benign response like acceptance or forgiveness or trying to learn from the incident. But for Turk, his reaction would be to extract revenge.

The file that Crane was apparently so concerned about was on the floor in the corner of Turk's cubicle. On top were a couple of medical bills he had been waiting to receive. He had actually received two of them a month ago. There was no urgency on this case other than the need to file updated reports in compliance with the company's arbitrary reporting guidelines. But Crane was technically correct; Turk's settlement evaluation report was late. Thanks to Crane, it now had the potential to be a stain on Turk's official record and adversely affect Smitty's opinion of him.

This situation required immediate and major damage control. The template for the liability/settlement evaluation report was on the computer. The claimant was Ms. Spendel, and the case involved a simple rear-end fender bender and mild whiplash. This case was low priority and insignificant, but nonetheless, like all claims, it was on the company's assembly-line reporting system. The idea, apparently, was that catastrophes and human suffering could be controlled and quantified from a financial perspective by a system of continuous reporting.

Turk completed the report in fifteen minutes. He called Ms. Spendel and, fortunately, she answered. He settled the case cheaply and scheduled an appointment to meet with her the next day to give her the check and have her sign the release of all claims form.

This had worked out perfectly. Now he would use his skills at revisionist documentation to bury the little sycophant who had dared try to one-up him in front of their new boss. Although the company conducted its work electronically on its vast computer network, it also maintained a paper copy, or hard copy, of each file that was the official file in the event the case went to court or the company received a subpoena. This was referred to as the master file. Although most communications were done by email, interoffice memos and reports were often done on paper and transmitted by interoffice mail or by simply putting the report on someone's desk.

Emails showed the date and time that they were sent. But this was not the case with interoffice reports and memos. The supposed date the memo was sent was the date written at the top of the page.

He backdated his report to two months earlier. In it, he requested $1,000 in authority so that his $800 settlement would look like outstanding, aggressive adjusting. He then typed a follow-up memo to Crane, which he backdated one month earlier. In it, he asked Crane if he had a chance to review his previous report requesting settlement authority. The claimant had called and seemed willing to settle. Turk didn't want to miss this opportunity. *Please advise.*

It was now quarter after five in the evening and everyone had left the office. Turk was ready to stick it to Crane. He went to the file room and made two copies of his report and follow-up memo. He located the master file and pulled it off the shelf. He sat down at the secretary's desk and hole punched the originals of the report and memo. He picked up the date stamp and, using the tip of his pen, adjusted the digits backward to match the dates of the reports. He stamped the reports with the red ink that noted the date under the word *received*. This would show that Crane had received the report and sent it back to the file room to be placed in the master file. Turk placed the report and follow-up memo in chronological order in the file, underneath the email from Smitty to Crane with a copy sent to the master file, asking for the status of the case. This must have been what prompted Crane's nasty email to Turk. Turk went back to his desk and typed another email.

> To: Stan Crane, Liability Supervisor
> From: Turk Malone, Sr. Claims Specialist
> Re: Spendel
>
> Claim no.: 52-A-903-SS
> Stan, thanks for your memo regarding the status of this case. This matter was on my calendar for follow-up. Didn't you get my settlement report or

follow-up memo? I wondered why I had not heard back from you. I have attached copies to this email in case you overlooked them.

I appreciate your efforts to move this case forward, but as part of the claims team, I have to ask myself if Stan could have handled this more efficiently? Wouldn't it have saved time for both of us, and for Mr. Smith, if you had just come to my desk and asked me about this? My cubicle is always open to my colleagues. Don't forget, effective communication is what sets American Security apart from its competitors.

Cc: with attachments: Allen S. Smith, Executive Vice President and Regional Claims Manager
Master File

Turk hit Send not once but three times. When Crane came in the next morning and read Turk's email, especially when he saw that a copy had been sent directly to Smitty, he would immediately run back to the file room and pull the master file. The reports would be there, properly punched, filed, and date-stamped. At that point, he would either doubt his own memory, question his perception of reality, or know that he had been had beaten by someone a dozen moves ahead, someone to be respected, someone to be feared, someone he should never fuck with again!

12

As Turk drove to Spendel's house, he pecked at the buttons on the radio, switching between stations, trying to find a song he liked. He caught the tail end of a commercial for a spray-on wrinkle remover and skipped to the next channel, but he had been exposed, the obnoxious tune continuing to bounce around in his head. He hated that tune, but he couldn't stop it from reverberating inside his mind. He didn't care that the spray-on could take out wrinkles in seconds without the need to iron. All of his clothes were permanent press. He knew they were trying to manipulate him, trying to get him to buy their products. With his intellect, he saw through it easily. But still, he couldn't get the tune out of his head. *Spray straight. You won't be late.* It kept repeating over and over.

Turk knew there was no psychic filter that could screen out the endless barrage of noise and crap he was exposed to before he had to process it, before it could affect him, before it could reach his subconscious mind. But after listening to countless self-help CDs, he had learned the technique of mind-cleansing rituals.

He had learned it from the award-winning series *Fight Back at Negativity: If You Don't Want to Think It, Erase It and Replace It.* Even though he had to watch the road, Turk tried to relax his muscles and put himself into a trancelike state. To help focus, he started repeating the magic phrase: "Out, out, damn spot. Out, out, damn spot." Coincidentally, this was also the slogan for a popular stain remover.

After about ten minutes, or maybe thirty minutes—Turk didn't know for sure—the technique seemed to have worked. Now, at this moment, his mind was a blank slate. The most important thing at this instant in time was that exposure to any stimulus be positive. Turk reached into his glove compartment and grabbed something inspirational. He didn't even have to look at the titles. His subconscious mind, now communing in harmony with the overarching superconsciousness that guided the entire universe, would pick the right tape for him. Turk needed only to let the superconscious flow through him as if he were an empty vessel being operated by remote control. The choice was *Goal-Setting Your Way to Success.* Of course. Turk popped the disc into the compact disc player.

"So many of us wander around every day aimlessly, as if we were lost in the wilderness. If you want to succeed, if you want to get from point A to point B, you have to set goals. You have to have a plan. Do you have a plan for your life?

And you have to be ready when you encounter hurdles. You also must have a plan to proactively engage in solution-focused problem redress …"

Turk had a plan all right, and he was moving toward his destiny—the realization of his PPP. After he made his utopia a reality, would they erect statutes of him? Would they find all the places he had left his mark—Turk—in cement and build shrines? Would people talk in Turkisms? Would future historians refer to this as the Turkmonian era? And what would the chimps be like after they had been pulled up one step higher in their development as a species? Would they be grateful? Would they honor Turk? Would they worship him as the first human to lead them on the path of developing to their full monkey potential? Would he become a new age demigod?

He met with Ms. Spendel, gave her the check, and had her sign the release. He drove home, exceeding the speed limits by precisely five miles per hour, the ultimate leeway he would expect any cop to give without pulling him over for speeding. He arrived at seven thirty and sat by the phone, waiting for Mr. Abdullah's call.

At eight o'clock, the phone rang.

"Hello, this is William Malone."

"Yes, Mr. Malone. This is Jaleel Abdullah. It is good to hear your voice." He spoke with a thick English accent and a deep baritone voice that resonated from his diaphragm. "I am calling regarding the mutually beneficial opportunity that you contacted us about. Yes, I do believe that with our contacts in Uganda we can secure for you twelve chimpanzees from the wild and sell them to you for a reasonable price."

"Thank you for getting back to me," said Turk. "Can you give me a ballpark estimate on what the cost would be?"

"I cannot lock myself into a final price at this time, but I am confident that we could deliver the chimpanzees to you, after shipping and handling costs and broker fees, for about $5,000 a chimp, for a total cost in the range of $60,000 to $70,000 dollars."

That seemed high to Turk, but he had researched recent jury verdicts for similar injuries that Brock had suffered and found several in the range of $100,000 to $150,000. Liability—that is, fault—was not an issue, only the amount of damages that Brock, his fictional claimant, had sustained. Turk thought he could easily get authority from Smitty to settle the case for at least $80,000 to $90,000.

"As we get closer, I'll need a firm number," said Turk. "But if you're confident that you can do it within that range, then I'm ready to move forward with this deal."

"Yes, I am confident in that price, sir."

"So what are our next steps?" Turk had learned to always end phone calls, meetings, and face-to-face conversations with this question from the well-known best seller on effective management techniques, *Next Steps to Success.*

"I think we need to meet face-to-face so that we can cement the bonds of mutual trust," responded Abdullah. "I am planning a business trip to the US in the near future. I propose that we meet in the city of Chicago. I believe that time is of the essence for both of us."

"Yes. That's fine."

"At our meeting, it will be necessary for you to tender to us a check in the amount of $10,000 as a down payment to cover our costs and expenses in securing the chimpanzees that you desire. Is that acceptable to you?"

Turk would never give them his checking account number, which would allow them to tap into his account and take everything. That was their scam, only they didn't know that Turk was aware of it. He knew he could not trust these guys and would have to be hypervigilant in his dealings with them. He needed to stay several steps ahead of them at all times.

"Yes and no," said Turk. "I'm happy to meet with you in Chicago and provide you with a down payment of $10,000, but it will be cash. All our transactions on this matter will be cash only."

"We are always amenable to dealing in cash transactions," said Abdullah.

Turk knew he could come up with $10,000 in cash by manipulating his credit cards or taking out a new credit card that offered balance transfers with no interest for up to twelve months. After he had implemented his PPP, he would have plenty of money to pay off all his credit card balances. He also knew that giving them the payment in cash would involve some risk; they could take the money and disappear. But it was less risky than the alternative. And they had an incentive to follow through on the deal. They stood to make another $50,000 to $60,000. Turk knew how these guys operated. They used their victims' own greed to lure them into their cons. But he was one step ahead. He would use their own greed to keep them in the deal. He was confident that he could beat them at their own game. He could outscam the scammers, outcheat the cheaters, and outhustle the hustlers.

13

The next weekend, he finished plans for another one of his projects, the Shitkicker. It was a portable toilet, not like the ones seen at huge events to accommodate masses of people but a smaller, personalized version. The toilet was modeled after ones used in RVs, but Turk's was light, easy to carry, and could be taken anywhere. What made the Shitkicker truly unique, though, was that it came with a small tent that could be quickly and easily set up to cover the customers as they sat on the toilet. They could enjoy complete privacy anytime, anywhere. This project had lain dormant as he focused his time on the PPP, but he wanted to close that loop. When he had more time, maybe he would revisit it.

The Shitkicker would be only one small part of a vast waste-disposal empire. Trash was the commodity of the future. As the planet grew, so did the need to dispose of the infinite variety of waste that people generated—industrial, medical, chemical, nuclear. It all had to be disposed of somewhere. Even the most basic human waste, urine and feces—that is, piss and shit—was a market of ever-expanding growth. According to the World Toilet Organization, the WTO, 40 percent of the world's population lived in such poverty that they had never flushed a toilet, at least a Western-style toilet.

The possibilities were limitless. Turk had just received his free copy of *The Scum Also Rises: Exciting Career Opportunities in Waste Management.* The first chapter, titled "The Trashman Cometh," was the remarkable story a high school dropout who started with nothing more than a used pickup truck and half a dozen rusty old barrels. From that humble beginning, through hard work and persistence, he built a company that brought in a net profit of more than $5 million a year with a fleet of trucks that hauled and disposed of industrial waste all over the country. For some of the truly hard-core chemicals like solvents, discarded coolants, refrigerants, and PCBs, he charged premium rates and the companies he worked with happily paid for the need that he had found and was filling.

The second chapter was "Creative Plumbing—a Metaphysical Approach."

The third chapter was titled "The History of Shit."

> According to sources on the internet, an "urban myth" circulated on the internet that the word *shit* came from ancient nautical practices. Manure was transported by ship in dry form, which weighed much less. At sea, if water contacted it, it became heavier. Also, the process of fermentation started, and one of the by-products was methane gas, which is highly explosive. As the methane began to build up in the decks below, the first time someone came down with a lantern caused an explosion. Several ships were destroyed before anyone discovered the cause and effect. After that, the bundles of manure were stamped with the term *SHIT*, which meant "ship high in transit," so that water would not touch the feces and start the production of methane.
>
> While this myth may have relevance to the history of the word, it does not describe its actual origin,

which dates back to the fourteenth century. The
word *shit* entered modern English derived from the
Old English noun *scite*, the Middle Low German
schite, and the Old English noun *scitte*, meaning
"diarrhea."

And there were so many other spin-off businesses. The market
was limitless—new age toilet design and sales, new age plumbing,
new age carpet cleaning, disaster recovery and cleaning, animal
toiletry. In addition, the advent of a new underclass of chimpanzees
to do human menial labor would in turn spawn an entire business to
ensure the proper and efficient disposal of monkey shit. Turk would
be in a position to be the first one to get a piece of all that action.

And then, of course, where would the chimps live? He would
start the venture by marketing to individuals for their own personal
monkey. But as that market developed, it would be obvious to
the heads of major corporations that there was a way to use these
monkeys to increase output, productivity, and profits. Turk could
easily change his business model to market to businesses of all sizes.
There would be no need to provide health insurance for these beasts.
Labor costs would be zero.

The only major expense would be the cost to house and feed
these domesticated primates. And Turk already knew the best and
cheapest way to fill that need was the housing of the future: mobile
homes. These animals would need only a basic level of subsistence.
Turk would develop a new type of stripped-down mobile home made
for a pack of chimps to live in, customized with modern monkey
toilets. Companies could build huge shantytowns of mobile homes
next to their factories to house the monkey population of workers.
The introduction of the PPP for human exploitation would create
an endless of cycle of needs and opportunities to fill those needs.

And what if his chimps could be used for the military? Could
Turk not develop chimps that could go into battle rather than

sending human beings? This could radically redefine the nature of war.

Before entering his house, Turk walked around to the backyard to check on the crickets. As he rounded the back corner, he could hear the high-pitched, annoying, screeching sound. This had been a truly great day. It was a beautiful clear evening in mid-October, one of the few remaining before the overcast skies and cold rains of November and the snow and bitter cold of winter.

14

Two weeks passed. Nothing different or exciting had happened, just more of the same. Turk still hadn't seen his kids. It was Halloween evening, and he recalled the times he had dressed them up in costumes. Once he had dressed up in some silly costume that he wore as they went door-to-door. They had loved it. He could remember wrestling on the carpet in the living room with the two of them. He would roll around, and they would jump on him and run around him and get all excited and laugh uncontrollably.

He knew trick-or-treaters might be coming to his door tonight. He wanted to avoid them. He had not bought any candy, and he didn't want to deal with the disconnect between then and now. He turned off all the lights that could be seen from the front of the house so it looked dark and unapproachable. Later that night, again, he could not fall asleep. It was two o'clock in the morning. Lying on the stand next to his bed was one of the magazines to which he subscribed, *The Journal of the American Association of Amateur Psychologists (AAAP): A Lay Person's Guide to Diagnosis, Treatment, and Self-Medication.* It was opened to an article titled "The Effects of Sleep Deprivation on Human Brain Function and Cognition." Turk started reading the article and then put it down. At that moment, he didn't have the energy to read and absorb the information about how his lack of sleep might be affecting him.

He picked up an article from the top of his stack of chimp research materials. It was about a theory that an AIDS-like epidemic killed a huge number of chimps around two million years ago and that this was why modern chimps were resistant to the AIDS virus.

Turk couldn't focus on what he was reading. He decided he needed to find out, if he went through with his insurance fraud scheme, exactly what laws he would be breaking and what the penalties were. This would not change his mind. He had already committed himself to following through with his plan. But he wanted to know up front how much prison time he might have to do if he got caught embezzling money from American Security. He thought he had created such an excellent alternative reality that he would never get caught and that he would be able to realize his dream with no repercussions.

But in case things didn't work out as planned, he also wanted to make sure he knew what the elements were of his crimes, what the prosecutor would have to prove. This might help him tailor his actions, maybe even set up some technicality or some abstract grounds for acquittal or appeal, even before he had completed his duplicity. This wasn't his idea; it was discussed in Felix's treatise, "A Metaphysical Approach to Crime." Turk had just put off doing this essential task that was needed in order to increase his chances of not getting caught or convicted.

He had learned a little bit about legal research at one of the training seminars for his job. American Security had an account that allowed its employees to do legal research online. This was set up for the legal department at corporate headquarters, but anyone could use it. He had a password, which he had never used. He had never tried to do a search before, but if Liz's lawyer was able to do it, it couldn't be that hard to figure out.

He logged onto his computer. He picked up the empty wrapper of a pack of powdered donuts and threw it into the wastebasket next to his desk. Then he brushed off the remnants of sugar onto the carpet. He searched for state laws. He knew there were also federal laws out there, but apparently American Security had only purchased the basic passage, which only included state statutes and case law. He clicked onto the criminal law section and browsed for crimes that would cover his contemplated actions. The first one he found was forgery.

> A person who, with intent to defraud, makes or utters a written instrument in such a manner that it purports to have been made (1) by another person; (2) at another time; (3) with different provisions; or (4) by authority of one who did not give authority, commits forgery, a class C felony.

There were probably other charges the prosecutor could file against him, but this one seemed to fit. He clicked the section on penalties. Forgery was a class C felony, and the penalty was four years, but could range from two to eight years, depending on aggravating or mitigating circumstances. He had all kinds of mitigating circumstances: it was his first offense, he needed the money to finance a project that could ultimately benefit the entire human race, he had kids, he wasn't dangerous, and it wasn't a violent crime. There were all sorts of excuses. With good-time credits in prison—two days for one—it was possible that he could be out in just one year, even if he got caught and convicted.

It didn't look like he could beat the charges completely, though. The elements looked pretty clear-cut. The only possible wiggle room he could see was that the crime required intent to defraud. Intent was a nebulous concept. If he resolved in his own mind right now, before he committed the crime, that he would pay back the money to American Security, did he truly intend to defraud? Just as soon as he made a profit, he would reimburse the company, anonymously, with interest pegged at 8 percent. Would this not be considered intent to borrow rather than intent to defraud?

Perhaps he was now operating on a different level to which the laws of humanoids did not directly apply. Except for the money, which he would pay back with interest, and the bank account, everything else about the scheme was fictitious. Were laws designed to deal with fictitious people who did not actually exist? The funds he would borrow from American Security would be diverted to a fictitious person and then to Turk, but he would ultimately return the money to the rightful owner. Did it not follow that he would be guilty at most of obtaining a short-term unauthorized loan?

15

On the way home from work the next evening, Turk decided to stop by the Mail Store. With all the ventures he was contemplating, he thought it would be best to channel all mail to this address rather than his home. It would be a buffer of protection in the event something went wrong. For instance, if anyone lost money on one of his opportunities or had a complaint, they could still track him down, but it would be more difficult. And now that he was preparing to actually commit a crime, it seemed like an even better idea.

It was almost dark. The sky was overcast, and the temperature had dropped. Just off the interstate on the southeast side of the city was a long stretch of strip malls and restaurants located on a four-lane highway. Turk was instantly transported, not into a time warp but a space warp. At that moment, Turk could be anywhere in the entire country, any city that had access to an interstate. He would be driving past the same restaurants, the same stores, the same gas stations, the same strip malls; everything would be the same. The only difference in this particular place was that the development of this stretch of business couldn't even reach the level of sameness as every place else. The owners couldn't even succeed at being the same. After about a mile, the landscape started to look barren. The strip centers were only half full. There were empty storefronts with signs advertising retail space available for lease. Even a large chain restaurant had failed. The sign had been removed, and the building was vacant. The area looked bleak and empty.

The car dealership with its neon signs beamed like an oasis of prosperity. Just past the used car lot was the entrance to a commercial industrial park. The Mail Store was located on the corner. It was the perfect place to set up a secret address. The place was open twenty-four hours a day, seven days a week. The entire front of the store appeared to be made of some type of bulletproof glass. Light poles were strategically placed to light up the entire parking lot. Inside, florescent lights illuminated every corner. The place seemed to glow, as if it had been zapped with a beam of radiation. This was obviously a safe place. It was too bright for petty crimes or physical crimes like robbery that were too risky to commit out in the open. Yet it was bland. It was well suited to the subtler transactions that he would be engaging in, which could be committed in broad daylight. In this place, he would not attract attention. It was open yet anonymous.

As he walked into the building, he felt an overwhelming certainty that he could be the key, the indispensable link to the future. He would lead humanoid kind into the next phase with his PPP. This could lead more broadly to the fusion of biology and technology. And who knew where it could go after that, perhaps microscopic computer chips implanted in the neuroelectrochemical circuitry of the brain to enhance human memory, intelligence, and consciousness? Turk was like that primal humanoid who picked up that first stick and began to use it like a tool or a weapon.

He opened his mailbox, and in it was a letter marked "return to sender." He had sent it to a vast worldwide corporation that manufactured soap along with its numerous other products. Apparently, they had not even opened it, just sent it back. They wouldn't even accept it. He was willing to share with them a revolutionary idea: soap that would lather in saltwater. But they had no interest. How could they be so shortsighted? This product was perfect for the beach. It was tailored to an entire market of surfers, swimmers, teenagers, and beach bums. It was a market waiting to be excavated like a deep vein of gold, yet there was no one with enough foresight to help him launch the project.

He had the ideas, the formulas; they had the money he needed to get these ventures started. He was willing to share what he had, and even risk that they might steal his plans. All he asked them to do was put up the capital. They had plenty of it. If they would just give him a little, he'd help them make a lot more of it.

He had not patented his product. So maybe they were going to steal it. And the best way to do that was not to leave any clues that they had ever received the letter. Best to seal it back up and return it as if they had never seen it, never read it, knew nothing about it. He inspected the envelope for signs that it had been opened, but there was no way he could tell. Obviously, these guys were pros. He opened the envelope and pulled out the letter. He skipped to the second page. There were the details of the perfect hair care product that found a need and then filled it.

> The primary ingredients in nearly all shampoos and soft soaps are sodium laureth sulfate and ammonia laurel sulfate. Good lather is an important characteristic rarely found in natural soaps. That is why the two sulfates are used.

> A few years ago, I traveled to Mexico to find a natural substance that could replace these chemicals. I chose Mexico because of its ancient Indian civilization. The Aztec people were extremely clean and incorporated hygiene into many spiritual ceremonies.

> I located a small factory that was sixty miles outside of Mexico City, toured the plant, and eventually

acquired the formula. The main ingredient is a coconut-based substance. When properly processed, the shampoo is a natural cleansing agent and lathers extremely well, even in saltwater, unlike current shampoos on the market.

He didn't get it. Of course, he had made up the part about the trip to Mexico, but they didn't know that. He figured that sitting in a corporate suite somewhere in the upper echelon of this company, there was probably some guy looking for that breakout product that could propel him to the top. When he saw this idea come across his desk, he probably jumped out of his chair with enthusiasm. He then made a copy of the letter, placed the original back into the envelope, and carefully sealed the edges of the envelope that had been ripped apart by the letter opener. How many times had this prick done it to others besides Turk?

Turk would monitor new hair care products coming onto the market. If this company came out with something like Sea Soap Shampoo, Surfer Gel, or Salt Lather Hair Care Products, he would know that his idea had been stolen. Maybe he wouldn't be able to do anything about it, but at least he would know. And this would provide even more proof that he had the potential to break out in a big way.

As he exited the parking lot, he had to veer around a huge pothole where the asphalt pavement had separated and then crumbled and deteriorated. Rather than head back the way he had come, he decided to drive in the opposite direction and take a tour of the light industrial office park.

For the first two blocks, the streets were alive with commerce. All manner of human needs had been found and were being filled. To his left was a huge neon sign that read, Creative Concepts in Floor Coverings. Next door was Opti-Clean and Dry—Carpet and Upholstery Specialists. Across the street was the home office of American Prosthetics and Medical Supply and ABC Electric.

Turk continued to drive past the row of businesses—restaurant supply, heating and air-conditioning, printing, auto repair, graphics design, and pool and patio installation—until he arrived at Son of the Carpenter—The Premier Outlet for Faith-Based Products. A neon sign on the front window read, Illuminati Frozen Pizza. Turk had been here before, but it was closed for the evening. He had purchased a tin container of Testamintos—handy breath mints wrapped in popular verses of scripture. And he had bought a small plastic statue of a cherubim, the winged angelic being placed in the garden of Eden to guard the path back to the tree of life. It had a suction cup on the bottom so that it could be mounted on the dashboard of a car, which was what Turk did. As he drove to and from work each day, and to accident scenes and homes of claimants, he had divine protection.

Turk recalled that the same day he had visited this outlet was also the last time he had seen his kids. It was in late August. Since then, every time it was his weekend to have them, something had come up at the last minute.

Liz had dropped them off at his house. She had said she would do some shopping and return later in the day. They had never seen his cricket farm. He had taken them to the back patio outside his basement and taken off the tarp that covered the vat of crickets. They had loved it.

When Liz returned later that afternoon to pick up the kids, Turk had invited her into the house and led her down to the basement and to the back patio. Alicia had been standing knee-deep in the vat of crickets. Nick had reached into the pit and pulled out a handful of crickets. He had run over to Liz and said, "Mommy, look what Daddy has! Isn't this cool?"

Liz had stiffened but hadn't responded. Turk had sensed that she was not pleased. He had seen this look of quiet disdain many times during their marriage.

"C'mon kids, it's getting late, and we need to get back home," she had said. "Bill, please hose down Alicia's legs. Nick, you need to wash your hands with soap."

Beyond Son of the Carpenter, the rest of the complex had been completely abandoned. The street sign read, Speed Limit—28 MPH. The buildings were empty, many of the signs were partially torn down, and the asphalt in the parking lots had deteriorated. As he maneuvered between the potholes in the road, Turk could feel a sense of loss. These were modern-day ruins, sprawling, decaying monuments to failure. Each deserted business represented someone's lost dreams. There was a negative energy to the place. It was like a sinkhole.

Turk pressed the accelerator and began to race down the street, bouncing as he hit potholes and swerving to avoid them. He had to get out of there. He could not get sucked in. He had to keep his focus. He would not make the same mistakes that they had made, whatever they were. He would not allow his mind to dwell on it. By listening constantly to his array of self-help CDs, he had programmed his thinking for success. He had developed the enhanced survival skills necessary to compete in the modern world, beyond those needed in the wilderness. He was moving forward.

16

After Turk got home from the Mail Store, he could not calm down. He went to bed, but again he couldn't fall asleep. At one o'clock in the morning, he gave up and went out for another late-night run. He knew this would affect him the next morning, as had happened many times before. He would sit in his cubicle, barely able to stay awake, writing reports while continually chugging cups of black coffee on an empty stomach as if hooked up to an IV, injecting straight caffeine into his veins.

Turk stood next to a high fence. Black metal rods rose from a three-foot high stone wall. He stared into the cemetery. It was pitch-black. He had parked his car on the street but didn't want to stray far from his vehicle. Turk was deep into the poorest, most destitute part of the city. The houses on the other side of the street were gutted; some were abandoned and boarded up. Even the poorest of the poor did not want to live here. The local nightly news often ran stories about terrible things that happened in this part of the city. People were murdered. There were drug houses and gangs. If Turk was caught down here, some slightly overweight middle-aged bourgeois from the suburbs, alone and in the dark, he would probably never make it back out.

He stared into the blackness in front of him. What lay beneath was the city's pauper cemetery. The graves were unmarked. This was where they buried the people who were so poor that they couldn't even afford to be buried. They didn't even have enough money to buy a small plot of dirt to die on and finish it out.

Here lay the poor, the unknown, the dead. Turk shined his flashlight into the darkness. The grave closest to him was smaller than the others. It was the only grave that had any type of marking. Someone had stuck a small sign at the head of the grave that read, Unborn Soul, indicating it was probably a stillborn baby or perhaps an aborted fetus.

All these beings had once been alive. Did it not follow that there was some meaning to their having existed? Did they still exist in spirit on some level, in some dimension? In heaven?

He went to work. He had his hammer and chisel. He worked fast. He was in the shadow of death. And he feared evil. After about three minutes, he stepped back and shined his flashlight on the stone wall just below the metal rods. It was there. He had left his mark for posterity. Thousands of years from now some future archeologist with sophisticated tools would discover it, standing in the same spot, gazing in the same direction that he did now, looking upon a vast discovery of unmarked graves. And at the entrance to the valley of the dead and the anonymous, his name would stand out—*Turk*. He was a witness.

17

Turk was back in his cubicle again. At least a couple of weeks had passed since his late-night run to the cemetery; he couldn't recall specifically. Thanksgiving was only a week away. He continued to have difficulty sleeping and each night stayed up into the early morning reading, researching, and working on his projects. It was as if he had been sleepwalking through his workdays, chugging cups of black coffee as each day blended into the next, each day the same as the one before or the one after. He still had not seen his kids. He and Liz had agreed to split the holidays. She would have the kids for Thanksgiving, and he would take them for an entire week during Christmas break.

Like every other morning, an unnatural smell emanated throughout his cubicle. This particular smell evoked a lost feeling. He couldn't figure out what it was, but it was pleasant, reassuring. Perhaps it touched off some buried memory of his grandmother baking homemade chocolate chip cookies. This was caused by Evelyn, a fellow adjuster in the cubicle next to him. She had seven candle holders. Three were placed in a row on the corner of her desk. The other four were placed on top of the file cabinet. Each one held a golden candlestick. Every morning when she arrived in the office, she lit the scented candles.

Evelyn had been with the company for something like fourteen years. She was middle-aged, overweight, and had three grown children. Her cubicle was covered with pictures of her offspring in various stages of their lives, from kindergarten to graduation, and her grandchildren. On her desk sat a large family portrait. Even though their workspaces adjoined each other, Turk rarely talked to her or interacted with her. She was pleasant enough but boring as hell.

He had tried to ignore it, but over time it had reached the point that he could no longer tolerate the candles. They were an insidious danger to the office. First, the scent was not contained to just her cube. It invaded his space. Evelyn, of all people—one of the most average and inconsequential people on the planet, in his view, although he tried not to be judgmental—was attempting to control his mood and behavior. Some people might not care. And most likely, she wasn't doing it consciously. But he did not get to choose the scent. She tried to create a cozy atmosphere. But he was not buying it. However docile she might seem; this was an attempt at mind control.

The first house fire case he had handled involved a candle that had been knocked over by some drunken lady when she passed out. The entire house had ignited in flames. One of the firefighters had made an incredible rescue and was able to drag her from the burning house.

While the pervasive scent apparently had the power to excite some chemical or electrical activity in his brain that could dredge up good memories and feelings, the potential ramifications were serious. If she could use these seven candles to affect Turk's mood and the moods of others near her cube and conjure positive feelings, did it not follow that she, or rather someone with sinister motives, could use this same device to manipulate people's feelings for more nefarious purposes?

There was no justification for the risk of maintaining small self-contained fires indoors. He was surprised that Smitty had not shut it down. So every night, Turk was forced to wait for Evelyn to leave so he could check and make sure that she had blown out the candles.

As a claims adjuster, he had seen countless people screw up and cause significant property damage or personal injury to others, or even themselves, sometimes just by forgetfulness or inattentiveness. Because of Evelyn's cavalier behavior with candles, Turk not only had to be careful to avoid making his own mistakes, but he also had to monitor Evelyn's actions to make sure she didn't burn down the entire office. He not only had to worry about the consequences of his own actions but her actions as well. He did not want to accept that responsibility, but he was the only one in the office who seemed to be aware of the danger posed by Evelyn.

He recalled Felix's essay on the power of focused, channeled thinking, "Thought Provocateur." The premise was that as humans continued to evolve and develop, they—or at least some of them—would someday discover the ability, using only their thoughts, to affect, alter, and change the physical world and the thoughts and actions of other people. This point in the future would later be regarded in history as the point in time when some humans had developed the ability to become demigods.

To some extent, this had already occurred. On a spiritual level, many people of different religions believed in the power of prayer to affect change in the physical world. On a physical level, an architect created the design for a building or a bridge, any type of physical structure, and ultimately it got built. Likewise, an engineer created an airbag that ultimately saved thousands of lives. Or perhaps on the flip side, the general of a vast army general commanded his troops into battle and ultimately defeated the enemy, although many people on both sides were killed. Or a physicist created the blueprint for an atomic bomb that ultimately killed thousands of people in one irrevocable instant.

It was Felix's belief that a direct power to affect change in the physical universe lay dormant within the human brain. And the first step in tapping into this vast, untamed potential was to simply acknowledge that it was possible. Since childhood, Turk had an intuitive sense that it was possible that he could change external events and people's actions by projecting his thoughts. It had not happened yet, but he thought it was, at least, a possibility.

Felix cautioned, however, that there were ramifications to accessing this type of power, so he warned that anyone who proceeded down this path should do so with caution. These demigod-like powers could be used for either good or evil, altruism or pure self-aggrandizement. Would any human being be able to handle that? Humans were not yet liberated from their evolutionary past; their minds were still subject to the warring factions inside their brains—the reptilian core and the higher executive functions that arose later.

Turk knew that he could not handle it. Whenever he smelled the scent of Evelyn's candles, his first thought was that he wanted to extinguish those flames. So if he did it with just his thoughts, she would not know how it happened, and she would light them again. And he would extinguish them again. And this scenario would be repeated until she gave up. But could it ever be a proper use of the power of thought to extinguish anything that was a source of light?

He had experienced occasions when he was growing up when negative, intrusive thoughts had burst into his mind spontaneously. He had not known where they came from. He might wish harm upon himself when he knew, both emotionally and rationally, that he did not mean to have those thoughts or intend for those thoughts to materialize in the real world. Nonetheless, since he believed that it was at least possible that he could control the external world with his thoughts, he would have to deal with the consequences that came with the exercise of that power, and for Turk, that was yet another burden that was too heavy to bear.

There was a period in early adolescence when these thoughts occurred frequently, and when it happened, he felt compelled to try to neutralize them. He would pray that he did not intend to think those thoughts and ask God to ignore them. He prayed that the thoughts would be neutralized in the past, present, and future, completely wiped out of existence as if they had never happened. He sometimes got lost in this ritual for maybe fifteen minutes at a time or more. Then, once the process concluded, another intrusive thought would materialize in his consciousness, and he would have to repeat the ritual again. This could go on for another half hour or maybe even an hour. He had no sense of time when this was happening.

The negative thoughts gradually receded as he grew into adulthood, but Turk knew he was not mentally stable enough to handle this power. He was afraid some random negative thought might pop into his head, something he did not intend, something he did not mean to think, and that he would not be able to control it. He would never intentionally harm himself or anyone else by his thoughts or actions. But he knew there were others out there who weren't as benevolent. And he was afraid that these people might gain access to this ability and use it not for the benefit of humanoid kind but for their own gain and self-interest. He did not know who they were or would be, but he knew they were out there. And Smitty was probably one of them.

18

This was beyond any lust and depravity Turk had ever seen or imagined! He had finally made it to the Lusty Loon Lodge. It was the weekend after Thanksgiving. One could only find such a place on the internet. The lodge was located on a compound in the center of a large tract of fenced-in land deep in a remote forest. There were hotel rooms upstairs above the bar and restaurant. The meals were all-you-can-eat buffets with a wide variety of meats.

On the website was an incredible offer for a weekend getaway: leave early Friday morning and return Sunday evening in time to get a good night's sleep and be back at the office on Monday morning after the ultimate weekend of "boozin', whorin', huntin', and killin'." It was advertised as "bestiality at its best!"

> During the day, you can experience nonstop killing and animal bloodshed, and at night, nonstop drinking, eating, and screwing. And we have only the classiest call girls. Go to machohunters. com to reserve the ultimate package deal— airfare, motel room, unlimited bullets, unlimited alcohol, unlimited food, and complimentary

prophylactics—for only $1,999. (Fornication costs not included. Void where prohibited by law.)

Turk was curious about what went on at a place like this. That was what had brought him here. He knew that very soon he would be living with chimpanzees in his basement, trying to convert them from wild animals to doppelgangers—doubles for their owners—chimps who could step into their places and do their jobs for them.

He wanted to experience the wild. And this place was deep in the primordial forest. So even though he didn't go out on hunting expeditions during the day, he watched, he observed, he learned. He was a witness.

The owner's business model was to create a captive forest stocked with deer so that people could pay to hunt and kill and, in such a controlled environment, be guaranteed to go home with a trophy that they could hang on the wall. For an additional fee, his staff would skin the deer, clean the meat off the bones, pack it up, and ship it to the guests. And the owner, a member of the class of the ultimate predator—that is, humans—had figured out other enticements—sex, booze, and gluttony—to exploit his guests' most base desires and make even more profit.

Next to Turk at the bar to his left were two stocky bearded men chugging shots of whiskey and guzzling beer. They slapped each other on the back as they laughed and shouted and made all types of loud, guttural noises. At a table in the corner sat a young woman in a short, tight black leather skirt. Her legs were spread apart. She was wearing bright red panties that clung tightly to her crotch.

A huge fat guy sat down next to her. He had a beer in each hand. He put one in front of her and then placed his hand on her bare white thigh. He had a tattoo of a coiled snake on his upper left arm. He had a huge potbelly. It looked like he had a bowling ball stuck under his T-shirt. It could not cover his mammoth belly. Just above the man's beltline, Turk could see folds of flesh around his waist that seemed to take on a life of their own. The guy turned toward the young woman, and Turk could see half of his butt crack. His pants barely fit over his sprawling hairy ass. Saliva and beer suds oozed down his face as he slobbered over her.

To Turk's right, a young woman stood completely nude from the waist up as she poured a beer into the wide-open mouth of some young stud leaning back in his chair. Mixed in with the smell of spilled beer and sweaty crotches was a musty odor that pervaded the entire place. It was the smell that arises from humans in heat. It was intoxicating.

After Turk got drunk, he wandered outside into the cold to see the heap of death. There was a huge pile of dead deer carcasses. The animals' eyes were still open. They stared back at him with blank, dark, dead eyes. Underneath was a large red puddle of blood that kept slowly expanding outward. The cold wind whipped into his face. He went back into the bar. The hunters had placed their rifles against the wall like golf clubs.

He didn't hunt. He didn't know how. He didn't even own a gun. But he had to admire the owner of the lodge. This individual had found not only needs but desires and had exploited them to make money. The difference between needs and desires was not always clear.

He didn't have the desire and thought it was cruel to take a weapon and kill an unarmed beast. Yet he knew he was a hypocrite because he was fine with letting other people slaughter cattle so that he could enjoy a steak or cheeseburger, and apparently these guys ate what they killed. But since the hunters had powerful weapons and the deer had only their ability to run away, Turk didn't understand how they could call it a sport. He also couldn't understand how they apparently enjoyed killing anything.

He had never been with a prostitute, so he had no frame of reference. But these were obviously really good ones. Still, who knew what diseases they might be carrying. So he was glad they had provided a complimentary packet of prophylactics. He had already stuffed one in his pants pocket so that he would be ready just in case. He pulled out the hermetically sealed packet and read the label: Jolly Poppers. Ribbed for Her Pleasure. At the top was a warning: "Do not open until ready to use." At the bottom was another: "After ejaculation, do not leave prophylactic inside vagina." That was certainly good advice.

Beautiful women sat at the bar and at the tables throughout the room. Turk had not gotten laid since the divorce, actually even longer than that, since the separation. He'd given the lodge his credit card number when he checked in, so the cost would simply be added to his room charge. There was no better time or place to give in to the desires of the flesh.

19

As he drove into the office the Monday morning after the Thanksgiving Day weekend, his penis was itching. He thought he may have experienced some pain when he took his morning piss. He had used the rubbers the hotel had supplied, but did they always work to prevent the transmission of sexually transmitted diseases?

At the exit to his subdivision was the No Right Turn on Red sign. He looked around to make sure there were no cops and then blew through the red light and pulled onto the highway, enjoying his civil disobedience as always.

Several minutes later, he pulled onto the entrance ramp to the interstate and then glided with ease into the maze of traffic. Once he had established his position, he reached down to the floor in front of the front passenger's seat and pulled up his case of compact discs. He began reviewing the titles:

Creative Incompetence
Unactualization, Part II: A Zen Guide to the Art of Sales
Live in a State of Spiritual Intoxication/Die Sober: Secret Tapes of
Alcoholics Anonymous (AA) Meetings
The Pass-Fail Approach to Life

Trivial Prayers
Shit Floats Downstream: A Manager's Guide to Effective Delegation

Turk located *The Compendium of the Writings of Felix.* His estate had continued to make money off his works after his death. They had made compact discs of each of his albums and also put all his writing onto a series of CDs. He popped the disc into the console. The treatise was titled "Find a Need, Then Fill That Need: The Ultimate Guide to Wealth and Happiness."

> Consider the concept of mulch. Imagine. Become rich by making a profit from the natural cycle of life—life, death, decay, and rebirth. Sell something to people that will not only fill their need but will eventually degenerate. To the extent that the supply of the product becomes empty, the demand becomes full. The market replenishes itself as the mulch degenerates into the earth, leaving a repeat customer with a limitless need to be filled. Profitable yet in tune with the natural rhythms of life and death.

> Consider also the simple concept of the parking garage. It is, after all, the most profound metaphysical, capitalist embodiment of the guiding principle that one must first find a need and then fill that need. How do we do it in this case? We make a profit off time, space, and location. The more time people spend in your space, the more money you make.

Turk had already listened to this entire discourse, so he repeatedly hit the Next button searching for another treatise. He came upon "Essay on the End Times" and "Essay on the Beginning Times: Back to Eden."

Turk hit the Play button.

> I have to admit that if I had been there in Adam and Eve's place and had been told that the one thing I absolutely could not do is eat the fruit of this particular tree, the tree of knowledge of good and evil, I would have been drawn powerlessly, obsessively, to that very thing that I was not supposed to do.

> And I would wonder, what happened to the tree of life? Is it still out there suspended in time? The cherubim and a fiery revolving sword were placed to guard the path back to it. So what happens if some Zen master, after years of deep meditation, transcends so far that he gets close? Do the cherubim start waving him off? And if he ignores them, then what? Does he experience a psychotic blowout?

Turk clicked the button to end the discourse. This was not the time to get sidetracked. He had to reign himself back in. He needed to keep pushing forward. The CDs had accomplished their purpose. He was motivated. Now he had to focus. He was ready to attack the day. Whatever happened, whatever curveballs life might throw his way today, they would be like Ping-Pong balls bouncing off him as he continued steadfastly on the path to his true destiny, the realization of the PPP.

The problem now would be concentrating on his boring job all day. He would be meeting with the Nigerian on Saturday. Turk had so many thoughts swirling in his mind. He had no appointments, just stacks of files that he had organized into neat piles according to their priority. This was another trick he had learned from one of the works in his extensive library of books and CDs—*Time Management for the Marginally Competent*. He had perfected these skills to such an art that he could organize things to the point that there was really very little he actually had to get done in any one particular day. Everything else could wait.

Once again, he had taken it to the next level, turned it on its head. His goal was not to be productive on his job but to do as little as possible, as little as he could get away with and still keep up the appearance that he was on top of things. The job was there to support him and his family, pay the bills, and support his crucial extracurricular activities.

His job security lay not in his productivity but in his ability to lie low, to avoid drawing attention to himself, and to hide within that broad range of mediocrity, that wide C+ to C– range that he had staked out so well as his turf when he was in high school and college. The time he freed up could then be devoted to his true calling in life. When it came to his ventures, he never put off until tomorrow what he could do today. When it came to his job, he never did anything today that could be put off until tomorrow. This was how one had to live among the petty bourgeois. These were basic survival skills.

Someday, after one of his ventures had caught on, most likely his PPP, he would publish his own self-help book. This would add even more money to his fortune. In it, he would share all his tricks with the oppressed and downtrodden, all those sleepwalking through their mundane lives. He would base it on the log he kept in which he continually recorded his techniques. It was titled *Exploits in Boredom*.

Turk pulled the file that was on top of his high-priority stack and began reviewing it. According to his filing system, at this moment, this was his most urgent piece of business that he had to complete. On top was a memo stating that he had an interim report that he had not submitted by the due date. But it was from Linda, and she was no stickler on deadlines. He could get that report to her anytime within the next week, and it would make no difference. What a system! Even the most important thing on his desk could be put off a little longer.

He could no longer focus on anything he was supposed to be doing. He had to get out of there. What was the point? He would only end up sitting immobilized in a timeless trance as he waited for his lunch break and then the end of the workday. He would lose another four to five hours of his life that he could never get back. He had followed his system so well that nothing was pressing. And though his job was vital and the foundation for supporting himself and meeting his obligations, with nothing in front of him that needed immediate attention, he wanted to spend time on his long-term priorities. But he also didn't want to get caught working on his own projects on company time.

He decided it was time to use one of the techniques from his work in progress, *Exploits in Boredom.* It was technique number seven: take advantage of global office computer calendars. Everyone in the office entered their appointments and meetings into the master office calendar. When scheduling appointments and meetings, one could see the calendar of everyone in the office. Turk believed management used their ability to view these calendars as a way to spy on the micromovements of employees. However, the schedule on the calendar was only the reflection of the data entered, not the underlying validity of that data. Therefore, the potential for manipulation was enormous. No one ever checked to see if an entry on the calendar corresponded with that activity on a specific file. That would be too cumbersome. So this was yet another opportunity to exploit the natural human tendencies of laziness, mediocrity, and incompetence.

In this instance, all he had to do was enter a bogus appointment on the calendar that would take him out of the office that afternoon. No one would question it. None of his bosses would expect to see him. He would be out of the office by one o'clock, and no one would expect him back before the end of the day.

When he arrived at his house, there was a package on the front porch. It was the starter kit for the diet plan he had purchased online, Live to Eat by Eating the Living. He opened up the package and read the instructional material.

> Welcome to your new revolutionary style of life! Enclosed is everything you need to start your new nutrition regimen on our patented step-by-step program, Live to Eat by Eating the Living! You will find inside the seeds you need to plant your garden of roots, sprouts, beans, and various vegetables; a vat to temporarily stock with live fish; a chopping board; and a razor-sharp knife with a serrated blade. You no longer have to eat processed foods or dead foods that are nutritionally depleted. You can connect directly with the life force that our distant ancestors thrived on as hunter-gatherers. Look at animals in the wild. This is the natural order of things.

> And you can bring this natural order into your very own kitchen. Just follow the simple directions. When you eat your freshly grown vegetables, eat them immediately after pulling them from the ground or off the vine. After you have stocked your vat with a living fish, pull it out of the water, flop it onto the cutting board, slice it open, and excise the portions you wish to eat. Skewer each portion with your fork, dip it into a pot of boiling water for just a few seconds to kill any germs, run it under cold tap water to cool it off quickly, and consume it in that instant.

> You are a living, vibrant being. Yet everything we eat is dead! We can't possibly get the life-sustaining energy that we need by eating dead food! The key is

to eat foods that are alive or very recently dead. The enzymes are still vibrant. The chemical processes of life are still in motion. Only by consuming the life force before it dissipates from our food can we energize and sustain the life force within us.

This was impressive. Turk was definitely glad he had purchased it during the special offer that included the chopping board and vat at no extra charge. But a lifestyle change of this magnitude would have to wait until the new year. That would be his New Year's resolution. He folded the package back up and placed it in his cabinet for future use.

20

The day to order his chimps had finally arrived, and he was sitting across from a middle-aged man with jet-black skin. He had shiny white teeth and eyes with deep dark pupils. A mosaic of red blood vessels, thick and inflamed, emanated outward from the black circles that were the centers of his eyes. His cheeks were puffy. He had a huge frame over which layers of fat had accumulated atop large bulging muscles that, once taut and powerful, were now atrophied and gradually degenerating into fat. On top of his head was a hat that resembled a cheerleader's megaphone turned upside down. A tassel hung from the side with an indecipherable emblem on the end.

Turk sat opposite him at a small Formica table that had been bolted to the floor and was precisely two feet from the heating unit underneath the window. The man was so huge he could barely squeeze himself under the table. Thick curtains hung from the top of the window. They were only partially open. The room was on the second floor and overlooked a parking lot.

It was mid-December, and a strong wind whipped against the window. Freezing rain and sleet pounded against the glass, which appeared to be thicker and more resilient than regular glass and allowed Turk to look directly into, while be protected from, the wild fury outside. Visibility was zero. He felt a tingling sensation deep in his belly.

The curtains were made of thick plastic. On the inside, a fabric had been snapped onto the back that matched the brown color of the room. These were no ordinary curtains. They were obviously the result of an elaborate manufacturing process. Some bright chemist had probably devoted years of his or her life to developing the compound, synthesizing something new and improved. These super-strength curtains could keep out any ray of light, real or artificial, at any time of day or night. They would last for generations. One could easily change the fabric on the inside to a different color or design to match the motel room and add a little variety, but the core of the curtains themselves would remain the same. They were easy to clean. They could simply be wiped down with soap and water. These curtains could be taken to the moon.

Although he had expected something fancier than a discount motel chain, the assembly-line room was clean, adequate, and indistinct, not the type of place where people engage in shady transactions. It was close to the airport. The stranger who purported to be from Nigeria, Jaleel Abdullah, had paid for the room. There would be no documentation that Turk was ever in this place. The day before, he had taken a cash advance of $9,950 on one of his credit cards. He wasn't sure about reporting requirements for credit card companies, but he knew banks had to report transactions over $10,000. So why take a chance? He had cash to cover the remaining fifty bucks.

And when he gave Mr. Abdullah the $10,000 in cash as a down payment, not only would he not need to disclose his bank account number, but there would be no evidence that this transaction had ever happened. He had nothing to hide. Still, there was no need to create a paper trail. Ambiguity was the key. With ambiguity came a lack of verifiability and with that, a lack of accountability and, ultimately, a possible way to dodge responsibility.

Turk was concerned, however, that his credit card debt was ballooning at an alarming pace, an obligation that he would not be able to obfuscate. He owed about $30,000 and was barely able to keep up with his monthly payments and child support.

"We are so glad you are on board with us, Mr. Malone," said Mr. Abdullah, his formal English accent enunciating each word precisely, as if compensating for a swollen tongue. "We do not normally engage in these types of transactions. Our goal is to transfer as much money out of the country as we can before Dr. Okaro leaves Nigeria and comes to the United States to form a government in exile. But when you presented us with this unique opportunity, we knew we had the means and the capability to fill the need that you have for chimpanzees and use the profits realized from this transaction to help further our cause.

"I'm sure you can understand the pressures we are under in our fight against the forces that would destroy our country. We must be ever vigilant. It starts with funding, obviously, which is the base, the foundation, for all our activities on behalf of the freedom and liberation of our oppressed countrymen.

"Dr. Okaro is a man of peace. He does not seek to cut off the head of the tyrant with weapons for another will surely grow in his place. Rather, steal his shoes. Then he cannot stand so tall. Take his money, and eventually, he will not have enough armor or weapons. Attack his base, force the roots to dry up and wither away, and divert those funds to water the seeds of progress.

"This is why I had to meet with you face-to-face, so I could look directly into your eyes. That is the only way to take the measure of a man, because all transactions of this nature must be grounded on a foundation of mutual trust and reciprocity. I can already see that we have found a man of the highest integrity, someone who can be trusted to keep his word and protect our confidences, a man of high intelligence, a man of great compassion and vision, a man willing to provide funding to our cause in our hour of greatest need."

Turk sat silent as he processed Abdullah's soliloquy. He had to admit, this guy was good. He had just met Turk and apparently was already convinced that he could be trusted. Although Turk knew that almost every word that came out of Abdullah's mouth was a compete fabrication, he had gotten one thing right. He had locked onto the true Turk. He could see something that his past teachers, coaches, and bosses had overlooked. He could see Turk for who he truly was, as well as the self-actualized Turk that he would become.

"You have found the right man," said Turk.

"I have no doubt of it," Abdullah said.

Turk pulled the $10,000 out of his backpack. He had sorted the hundred-dollar bills into ten separate stacks and wrapped each one with a rubber band so that he had ten packets of $1,000. He counted out each packet as he laid it on the table. Abdullah jerked backward as if seeing that much money in front of him in pure cash had almost triggered the onset of a seizure.

"Yes, Mr. Malone. We have found the right man."

21

That evening on his return, he stopped at a church about a mile from his house. The Nigerian had nailed it. Turk was, indeed, the *right man*, in the right place, at the right time. He was the quintessential right man to bring about the realization of the PPP. He had developed a way to finance the project through his embezzlement scheme and a way to procure the chimps by initiating contact with players in a vast underclass.

It was two o'clock in the morning. The name of the church was on the front of the building, but he didn't notice it. It simply escaped his attention. He was focused on something else. So if someone asked him where he had been that evening, he could answer truthfully that he did not remember the name of the church, because it never registered in his consciousness.

He was aware that he, like everyone else, probably filtered his perception of reality through his own subconscious predisposition, biases, genetic makeup, and experiences. First, he was limited by the human form. He was able to perceive and experience only a limited fragment of the total spectrum of existence at any one moment and only in a series of continuous, isolated moments strung together in chronological order—that is, in time.

Second, even within that realm, he could only process so much at once. Of those things that he physically had the ability to perceive and experience, he still missed a lot. There were things he simply observed, other things he paid no attention to, and certain experiences he obsessed on, like Liz's rejection of him. And some parts of the reality that he did perceive and experience, he forgot or rationalized. He was only able to get an obscure glimpse of a tiny slice.

It wasn't even possible that he could have knowledge of all that was objectively known through science, math, physics, history, media accounts of current events, and his own observations. There was simply too much out there. And much of science and physics was theoretical. Moreover, all the sources of objective reality were ultimately the work of humans susceptible to his same limitations. And overlaying this was the possibility of the supernatural—an order of existence beyond the visible, observable universe.

So essentially, he was existentially lost. He had gained the knowledge that there were things he simply didn't know and the awareness that there were things of which he was not aware. And if he was right, it meant there could be forces out there that he wasn't aware of that could be controlling him, affecting his thoughts, his feelings, and ultimately, his behavior, or maybe not. Or perhaps even worse, what affected his life could be simply a random confluence of events. So even though he wanted to be able to control his life and his destiny, it was probably beyond his control.

He had purchased the award-winning series *Take Charge of Your Subconscious Mind: You Are What You Think,* which he thought could provide him some defense, although he had not yet had time to listen to it. On the packaging it promised to teach him how to make a conscious effort to choose what he perceived, observe what he wanted, and tune out the background noise and negativity. He would learn how to tap into his subconscious and project his intention into the broader collective consciousness that would intuitively guide him toward the realization of his goals and guide him to make the right decisions and choices in his everyday life.

In front of the church was a statue of a saint. Turk didn't know which one. To him, they were interchangeable. By becoming saints, although now famous throughout history, they had given up all sense of ego and self-pride. Turk, however, knew that he was not so enlightened. Next to the pedestal on which the statue stood was a large concrete flowerpot filed with dirt. He bent over and pushed it to the side. It was heavy, but he was able to move it over a couple of feet.

There in the concrete, just as he had imprinted it in the cement years ago using only a branch he had found lying nearby, just how it had looked then even before it had dried, just how it looked now, and just how it would look in the future, was his mark etched in concrete—*Turk*.

22

As Turk drove into the office on Monday morning, he could not stop thinking about the confluence of opportunities he had created and set into motion. So many things were coming together at this historic moment in his life, and possibly that of all humanoid kind, with each step closer to the realization of the PPP. He had stuck with the program, and now it was paying dividends. He once again blew through the stoplight with the No Right Turn on Red sign, unable to contain a smirk as he flouted authority once again.

Near his office, he passed the Wily Rascal's Pub that was just around the corner. It was closed now, but every evening as he drove home, he could see that the place was packed. The parking lot was always full. In warm weather, people would sit outside. He had never stopped and gone in, afraid he might see someone from the office and be forced to have a superficial chat. But he kept thinking that someday, when he felt up to it, he would go in. It seemed like everyone in the place was so jolly all the time. He figured something had to be going on in there, something exciting, something exhilarating, something missing from his own life.

He gulped another drink of coffee from the plastic mug he had that was specifically designed for people to drink coffee and drive.

His mind was racing. He knew this would be an exciting week following an incredibly productive weekend. After his meeting with the Nigerian and his trip to the local church, he had slept only a few hours on Saturday night as his sugar-and-caffeine high carried him early into the morning. On Sunday, he had binged nonstop on microwavable meals and snack foods. During this time, he had made even more progress on the PPP.

He had developed a marketing strategy and had also written the initial advertisements. He would start by placing mini billboard ads over urinals in men's restrooms. He would catch them while he had their attention. He'd get his message right in their face:

Tired of pissing your life away?

Bored?

Tired of carrying the monkey on your back?

Why should you have to work? Send the monkey in your place. Let the monkey do the work. All you have to do is collect the money and take care of your monkey!

Interested?

Call Turk

It would be a nationwide blitz. Every stall in every restroom across the country would carry his utopian message.

After Turk got settled in at his cubicle, he pulled the top file off the stack on the corner of his desk. He opened the file to see what task lay ahead. An interim status report was due in two days. That would be a mind-numbing activity. But it could be put off another day or two, as long as he met the deadline. He grabbed the next file on the stack. On that claim, he needed to dictate a follow-up letter. In the file below that, a check needed to be processed. Nothing here was urgent. He was certain that every other task in the pile of files on his desk was equally boring and less pressing.

Unlike butthole Crane, who had files spread everywhere around his cubicle, Turk was organized. One of the handiest tricks he had developed was technique twenty-one from his work in progress, *Exploits in Boredom.* One of the tasks necessary on every personal injury file was to obtain the claimant's medical records. In order to obtain these records, it was necessary for the claimant to sign and return authorization forms.

All letters sent from the office were supposed to be sent on company letterhead, which had the address and phone number at the top. The form letter also stated that a postage prepaid envelope was enclosed. So whenever Turk sent authorization forms to a claimant, he never included a return envelope. He always made two copies. The letter he sent to the claimant was on blank paper with no letterhead. The copy saved to the file was on company letterhead. The letter stated that the authorizations were enclosed. Turk never enclosed them. The letter instructed the claimant to mail the authorizations back to the address listed above. There was no address. In the closing paragraph, the claimant was advised to call him at the number listed above with any questions. There was no number.

While many determined or resourceful people could figure out a way to get their claim moving forward and get those signed authorization forms back to him, there were many others—the confused, the lazy, the ones who were batshit crazy or just plain stupid—who could never figure it out. In thirty days, Turk would send a follow-up letter, again on blank paper. And again, the copy placed in the file was on letterhead. Would they please return the signed authorization forms he had sent them a month ago?

He put a reminder on his calendar to follow up in another thirty days. This time he would finally print the correspondence on letterhead and enclose the authorization forms. Would they please sign and return this third set? He needed their cooperation to resolve their claim in a timely manner. Turk would then send a memo to his immediate supervisor advising that the claimant had not been cooperating and all reporting deadlines would have to be pushed back ninety days. He had successfully used this technique countless times. And on each file, he had bought himself time, an extra three months, to procrastinate and, just as importantly, circumvent the company's reporting guidelines. Yeah, he was sticking it to the Man!

Turk stared at the pictures of Nick and Alicia. God, it had been a long time since he had seen them. But it wouldn't be long until he would get to spend a lot of quality time with them over Christmas. Perhaps the quality of the time could make up for the lack of quantity. He was concerned that a new pattern was being established in which he was becoming irrelevant and expendable, except when it came to paying child support. Liz and the kids were carrying on with their lives without him. He knew that he and Liz would probably never reconcile, but had he also lost his kids?

Since there was nothing on his desk that he had to do immediately, he decided he would glance at the newspaper and then tend to some personal business. He pulled from his briefcase a notice he had received for a late credit card payment. This was one of his three credit cards, the only one that was paid off. He had just taken the $9,950 advance on one of the other two credit cards, so he was now close to his limit on both cards. This was the card he used to get cash advances to pay the minimum balances due on his other cards.

He had previously paid the balance in full, but according to their records, the payment was received a day late. Now he owed a twenty-five-dollar late fee. And on top of that, they jacked up his interest rate permanently. He knew that if he did not pay this bill immediately, he would be hit with another late fee, and he would have to pay interest at a higher rate on a balance that consisted of only late fees on a bill that he had already paid in full.

This was all apparently legal. He had signed the credit card agreement without reading it. This must have been in the fine print. The problem was that it seemed like the due dates kept getting shorter. He never had thirty days anymore, and none of his bills were ever due on the first or fifteenth of the month when he routinely paid his bills. He refused to take the time to pay each bill separately as it arrived. He was busy and had more important things to think about. He routinely paid his bills once a month. But that wasn't possible anymore. They were controlling his behavior and, in so doing, his mind. As he contemplated the notice, he started to get pissed off about how they had screwed him.

But what really pissed him off was the thought that someone, probably someone with a master's degree in business administration, or maybe someone with an MBA and a law degree, had put a lot of thought into this. This overpaid prick had figured it all out—how to put people, without their actual knowledge but who sort of knew or maybe should have realized, on this endless financial treadmill and force them to just keep digging deeper into their pocketbooks, a little more at a time, burying them deeper into debt. Instead of using his or her education and talent to help end world hunger or do something noble, this was what the smug little asshole was up to.

And even more frustrating than being blindly manipulated by this ubiquitous figure was that Turk knew that, given the opportunity, he would probably accept a job like that to get paid huge sums of money to figure out how to exploit human weaknesses and incompetence. This was probably the same guy, or some other arrogant clone, who had developed the arbitrary reporting system for Turk's claims department—a diabolical genius who had gone light-years beyond simply finding a need and then filling that need. This guy had found a need and then exploited that need, distorted that need, created dependence, and in turn, created not just a new pseudoneed but a requirement. And this arbitrary pseudorequirement, which Turk had signed off on when he applied for the credit card and accepted the boilerplate terms, went beyond any need he had at the time but was now legally binding.

This guy had to be in the same class as those unrepented souls who wrote advertisements promoting cigarettes, booze, gambling, overspending on material possessions—anything preying on humans' tendency toward addiction—or who wrote distorted political attack ads, the new age, neo-Nazi propagandists. In the extreme, these were the people who developed ever more sophisticated weapons. In the more banal and benign forms, as Turk saw in his job every day, they were the attorneys and chiropractors who colluded to create inflated medical bills for pseudomedical care so that they could collect real money on claims for pseudoinjuries. They were tax attorneys who lived in a netherworld of manufactured, self-perpetuating complexity that fed upon itself and, in the process, resulted in huge legal fees.

At some point, they must have crossed the line and started believing the lie. And Smitty was one of these people. They weren't criminals but, with this mindset, were multiple levels more sinister. They were not officers in the regular army. These people were SS. Unfortunately for Turk, he had no choice but to pay this bill, although it consisted of nothing more than late fees because of his inability to adhere to artificially created deadlines.

23

Turk could see the young woman standing behind the counter. It was eight fifteen on Tuesday morning. He had stopped for a quick breakfast at the fast-food restaurant near his office and there she was. She had deep, dark eyes and long black hair that set off an angelic face, a face like a Madonna with a few pimples on her cheeks. She could have just stepped out of a Renaissance painting or the cover of a glamor magazine and into her position behind the cash register. She was timeless. She was a young goddess with pimples and newly sprouted boobs.

She moved gracefully from the fryers to the coffee machine. Her jeans clung like elastic around her tight buttocks and into her butt crack. Her bra squeezed her breasts upward above her white apron. Her clothing barely concealed her true proportions. Turk could see the outline of her nipples. Her bra strap, exposed, hung down over her right shoulder. She could not contain her sexuality. She was busting out. She was young. She was cellulite-less. She was blooming.

Even as he was mesmerized by youthful beauty, Turk could envision a complete staff of chimps behind the counter. They could do everything. They would fry the burgers, dump the wire baskets of fries, and eventually even work the cash registers. After all, with the computerized cash register, they didn't have to be able to add and subtract. The computer would tell them how much change to give. All they had to do was be able to count from one to ten. Turk was confident that eventually he could take his chimps to that level. He would need maybe one human behind the counter to direct the entire operation.

All he needed to do was design a system where every step was broken down to its most basic elements. Make it simple, step-by-step. He would then be ready to interface his sophisticated modern equipment with his highly trained chimps on the cutting edge of monkey-primate intelligence.

Some might argue, why not just go robotic? Turk was fine with that and with anything that would free humans from the drudgery of menial labor. He planned to offer another option. In the future, people would have alternatives to choose from or perhaps could use both at the same time. The use of primates injected another element of flexibility and adaptability. Perhaps chimp development and technological innovations would evolve together, synergistically playing off each other. Turk's dream was the merger of the highest human technology with the most highly developed primate skills. And there was a connection between human and chimps that did not exist with robots; there was flesh and blood and DNA.

As he completed the purchase of his breakfast, he realized that he was way out there now, maybe getting a little bit loony but not in a scary way. He envisioned the PPP. He saw it. He could make it a reality.

When he returned to the same fast-food restaurant later that day for lunch, his Madonna was no longer there. Instead, another young woman had come on shift and stood behind the same cash register. She was ready to take his order.

"May I help you?" she asked softly. She did not look up at him.

She had a name tag pinned on her uniform that read, Debbie Hostein. But what was different about his encounter with this young woman was that she was guilty, although not in Turk's eyes, of the ultimate sin. For this, kids would make fun of her at school. People would avoid her. Some would express hateful comments toward her. She would be isolated and lonely her entire life. She would probably never get married. As she got older, it would matter less as everyone else started to catch up with her as they slowly withered away. She must have somehow gotten stuck in the backwater of the gene pool.

She was ugly. And she was not just unattractive. She was grossly obese and butt-ugly. The pockmarked, acne-scarred skin on her cheeks appeared to have the texture of some old fart's hairy, pimpled buttocks. She had tried to cover up her poor complexion with heavy makeup, but it didn't work. She was the cellulite queen. The smell of deodorant was thick. Her skin looked pasty like she was malnourished or maybe had some type of chemical imbalance.

Turk felt so bad for her, but he just had to look away.

24

After lunch, Turk had a property damage claim he had to investigate. The claimant reported that vandals had broken into his mobile home and stolen his guns. To purchase insurance on firearms, one had to have a special rider and pay an additional premium. This guy had not listed the three assault rifles he claimed had been stolen. He lived in a trailer park about twenty miles north of the city.

Outside the mobile home was a new pickup truck, clean and polished, with a gun rack mounted behind the cab. Turk knocked on the door. Although he had talked with the claimant by phone and scheduled the appointment, there was no response. He knocked again even harder and could detect some rumbling inside.

Eventually, the claimant opened the door. He was young, extremely thin, and wearing only a tight pair of jeans and no shirt. He had tattoos on his upper arms. Turk could see the outline of his rib cage. His skin was white like an albino. His eyes were opaque. His long blond hair was matted down on top and hung unevenly above his shoulders. He had blond stubble on his face.

"Hi. I'm Bill Malone," said Turk. "As we discussed on the phone, I'm here to talk about your insurance claim." Turk would usually give the claimant his business card but decided not to do so this time.

"Yeah," replied the claimant. "Come on in."

Turk walked through the entrance of the mobile home. The place was small and packed with dead animals. There were several stuffed deer heads mounted on the walls. In the corner was a huge stuffed black bear standing on its hind legs. Its mouth was wide open, with long, sharp teeth. It was frozen, motionless, and thankfully for Turk, dead. Turk felt a tingling sensation deep in his belly. He was crammed into this small place. Would he be able to make a quick exit if necessary and run away, or would he be trapped in this cramped, stifling room? This guy obviously loved to kill. Could this extend beyond the animal kingdom to humans? Would the next head mounted on the wall be Turk's?

His first instinct was to run. But he was a professional. Within seconds, he had composed himself. They sat down at the kitchen table. Behind the claimant on the wall hung pictures in which he was holding up carcasses of even more dead animals.

Turk knew from the file that the claimant worked in a warehouse as a forklift driver and made good money for someone with no college education or specialized skills. Turk also knew the trailer couldn't be worth much. Yet lying on the table was the most recent cell phone on the market. Against the wall facing Turk was a mammoth flat-screen television that was almost as high as the ceiling and easily six to eight feet wide. When the claimant turned it on, whatever was on the TV screen would overwhelm the objective reality in the room.

This guy was the opposite of Turk's grand scheme, the Primo-Primate Project, the PPP. This guy was retro-evolutionary. He was going backward. He was devolving. He was ppp—piss poor protoplasm.

"So what was stolen?" asked Turk.

"A pistol, a hunting rifle, and three semiautomatic rifles," the claimant said.

"So I assume you like to hunt?" asked Turk.

The guy nodded in the affirmative.

"I assume that you don't use the semiautomatic weapons for hunting?"

"That's right."

"I mean, what would be the sport in that?"

The claimant did not respond.

"I know this isn't any of my business, but why do you own semiautomatic weapons?" Turk knew this had no relevance to the claim, but he felt compelled to ask.

The claimant paused and then said, "You are right. It's not any of your damn business. But I'll tell you anyway. Self-protection."

Turk knew he should stop before the claimant got angry but again felt compelled to ask.

"You need three military-style assault weapons to protect you from what?"

The claimant paused again. "It's a dangerous world out there."

Turk pulled the rider out of his briefcase. As he reviewed it, he confirmed that the three semiautomatic rifles were not listed on it. He knew this would cause a coverage problem, because each weapon, along with its serial number, had to be listed.

"When did you purchase these?" asked Turk.

"I don't know. Maybe six or seven months ago," said the claimant.

"Did you contact American Security and report the purchase?"

"No. Nobody told me I needed to."

This was not exactly true. The rider stated that only the listed items were insured. Any additional purchases would increase the premium and had to be reported to the company to have coverage.

"Is there some kind of problem?" asked the claimant.

Turk could sense by the tone of his voice that he was getting agitated.

"No problem," Turk said. He closed his briefcase, stood up, and moved quickly toward the door. "You'll hear from us within seven to ten business days," he said as he exited the trailer.

He walked swiftly to his car. He was not going to have a conversation about lack of coverage with this lowlife in his creepy mobile home with no clear means of escape. He would go back to the office and send the guy a check for the pistol and hunting rifle along with a denial letter for the assault rifles.

The claimant would probably get angry about the denial. Thankfully, Turk had not given him his business card. And when Turk sent the letter, he would not include his name at the bottom of the letter. It would state simply, Claim Department.

As he drove to his house—without his ex-wife and kids, he was so alone that he couldn't consider it his *home*, just his *house*—Turk put another of Felix's CDs into the console. It was titled, *The Metaphysics of String Theory and Parallel Dimensions*. Turk kept punching the button until he got to the chapter titled, "String Theory, Parallel Dimensions, and the Meaning of Suffering."

> Physicists who advocate string theory think that there are ten or possibly eleven parallel dimensions. Each dimension exists alongside the others like strings on a guitar. They are all interrelated and dependent on each other. This is the finely tuned balance of the universe. The lowest E string correlates with the Hindu word *Om*, and like an electric guitar, when the strings of these dimensions are strummed together, they harmonize and sync with a creative force that resonates throughout the universe.
>
> However, if even one of these parallel dimensions did not exist, the entire universe would collapse in upon itself and cease to be. We would cease to be. All creation would not exist, would never have existed in the past, and would never exist in the future.

Ultimately, this is the meaning behind our suffering. The existence of the universe depends on it. It depends on us. Without the life, death, pain, and suffering that we experience in this dimension, in our physical realm of being, the universe would not exist, it would not be, we would not be. There would be only nothingness, only a dark, formless, limitless void.

So my question is if it is possible that there is a parallel dimension that is purely spiritual in nature, and if that spiritual dimension were to merge with our physical one, would that be sufficient to support the existence of the universe without the need for the pain, suffering, and death that we experience in this dimension?

25

Turk woke up in a great mood the next day. Christmas would be here soon, and he would finally get to spend time with his kids. He arrived in the office early and placed the hard copy of his liability/settlement evaluation report for Mahone's claim against Brock in Smitty's in-box. He then went to his cubicle and sent Smitty an email with a copy of the report attached. It was December 18, two days ahead of the deadline. Again, he demonstrated outstanding compliance with the company's reporting deadlines.

He increased Mahone's permanent partial impairment rating and added another course of physical therapy. He asked for settlement authority up to $80,000. He stated that he had some preliminary discussions with the claimant and was certain that he would accept that amount in full settlement of his claim. This would give Turk the $70,000 he needed to complete the purchase of the chimps and also allow him to reimburse himself for the $10,000 he had already paid to the Nigerians.

Turk logged onto his cell phone to check his text messages. There was one from Liz. He clicked on the message. She was probably providing him with the specifics of the drop-off.

Dear Bill:

I know how much you have been looking forward to spending Christmas break with the kids. However, something just came up that I wanted to ask you about. My parents have invited me and the kids to spend Christmas vacation with them down in Florida. They have offered to pay the airfare and everything.

I know I promised you the kids over Christmas, and you can hold me to it. I haven't told the kids yet. But I do think it would be great fun for them. And they could spend some quality time with their grandparents. You can say no, and I will understand.

But if you could see it in your heart to let them go, I will be sure that they come spend the weekend with you as soon as they get back and that you can have them for the entire spring break.

Please let me know. I tried to call several times but got your answering machine.

Thanks.
Liz

Turk had to give Liz some credit; she knew how to get what she wanted. He missed Nick and Alicia so much, but how could he interfere with these plans? And her counterproposal was reasonable. He had to put the happiness of his children above his own. Besides, he was so preoccupied with the next steps of his PPP; it might be better to wait until spring break when he could have them for an entire week and focus all his thoughts and attention on being with his kids. He replied as follows:

Dear Liz:

I received your text requesting permission to take the kids to Florida for Christmas break. Although I will miss them terribly, I cannot in good conscience stand in the way of what should be such a wonderful experience for them. Take them south with my blessing and give them both a big kiss and hug from me. Start building them up about how much fun spring break will be.

Bill

At that moment, Turk felt noble. He was engaging in one of the few truly selfless acts that he had ever committed in his entire life. He was sacrificing his own wants, needs, and desires for the happiness of his kids. And he did this even though he ached to be with them and desperately wanted to be an intact family again, Bill and Liz together with their two children.

Before the separation and ultimately the divorce, he had been a good father. He still was, or could be, if he could reconnect with his kids. By all appearances, he thought he was pulling it off and that everyone thought he was a normal guy. And by any objective, measurable standard, he thought he was. But regardless of any of that, he was very involved in the lives of his children. He had always been there at every event at school, at every parent-teacher conference, at every game. He had even coached Nick's soccer team one season. Well, technically he was the assistant coach, but he was still a coach, nonetheless.

After the separation came the isolation and loneliness. Yes, it freed up more time for him to work on his projects and, finally, the PPP. But his life as it had once been and his sense of himself in that paradigm was slipping away. And it was getting more difficult to envision any scenario where he might be able to get it back. He was sinking. He should have been able to move on with his life, but he hadn't been able to do it.

26

The entire period from Christmas through New Year's Eve was a blur. Many people in the office took time off around the holidays. Turk had scheduled vacation time, but after the text from Liz, he submitted the required memo canceling that request. He always hated taking any of his vacation time around Christmas anyway. It was actually the best time to work. Nobody was around. Nothing got done. It was a great time to log in workdays without having to do much of anything. He could save his time off for when it really counted.

Liz's last-minute change of plans upset Turk's parents. When he got together with them and his brother on Christmas afternoon, he had to explain why the kids were not there. He should have called them in advance. They looked so disappointed. They had two huge gift-wrapped boxes. They left them with Turk. He was sure each one contained something truly extraordinary.

According to his mother, Turk's problem was that he was just "too willing to cave to that little b—Never mind, I won't say it." He needed to "stand up for himself." That's what Turk thought his mother had said. But now he couldn't remember whether she had said it or whether he had dreamed that she had said it or whether that was what his brother had told him she had said. It was also possible that she had said it a long time ago and he had forgotten it, but then his brother reminded him that she had said it before or again, and although he had once forgotten it, he now remembered it. It was all a blur.

Once he'd had kids, Turk gave up on the idea that he could blame his parents for all his problems. He didn't want Nick and Alicia someday to blame him for their unhappiness. He wouldn't be able to get out of it by simply pointing a finger in the direction of their grandparents.

The thing was, somewhere he had gotten the idea that as he got older, he would get wiser. He would learn from his mistakes. Somehow he would gradually figure things out. There would have been an underlying purpose to all his suffering. He would find peace of mind and understanding. He would pass this knowledge, accumulated over years of hard-fought experience, down to his children, who would benefit from his insight and wisdom. They would not have to make the same mistakes.

But things didn't seem to be going that way. He was like so many claimants he had met. Somewhere along the way, they had slipped; they made a big mistake, or maybe a lot of little ones, things got off track, and everything snowballed. The stories were similar. They had a lot of debt and issues with their spouses, kids, bosses, whoever. They had lost a job or were going through a divorce. Often drinking or drugs were involved.

Sometimes they got hit with a minor traffic offense or a misdemeanor charge but didn't have the money to pay the court costs and fees. So those costs multiplied and mounted up. These poor souls were now on a treadmill that kept getting faster, and the weight of what they were carrying on their backs kept getting heavier. So they turned to credit cards or payday loans, but this pattern kept repeating itself. And at some point, they fell off. But the fees and penalties kept accruing. Whatever it was, they just couldn't dig themselves out of it. And perhaps Turk was one of them.

Turk could see himself someday sitting alone in a chair in a nursing home, old and frail, unable to care for himself, closing in on the end, staring out the window with nothing to do but think back on his life and wait to die. And what would he be thinking? Would he even be able to think clearly? Was it possible that he had already died but did not know it and that he was actually in hell at this moment? Was it possible that one didn't have to die to be in hell? Could he have gone straight to hell without stopping to die, just a straight shot to hell on earth? He didn't know, but at this moment, it felt like it.

He felt he must have got it all backward, worrying so much about every little detail, every contingency, rather than taking a broader view. He worried about the small particulars, the minutiae. Did it really matter? Or was he being too hard on himself? After all, there was a universe big and small, infinite and microscopic. As Felix wrote in his treatise "The Mighty Mitochondria":

> Mitochondria in our cells are microscopic, and what they are and their function are not known to us, except from scientific observation. It is not something that we consciously perceive or are aware of, even though it takes place inside our bodies. But if the mitochondria did not do their job, we would all be screwed. Nothing would work right.
>
> So are your day-to-day activities any less important in the grand scheme of things than the actions of the mitochondria and all the other life processes occurring at this moment in your body and at other levels of existence? The human activities of working, supporting a family, contributing to the endless economic cycle, eating, pissing, shitting, fucking, procreating, surviving, living—aren't these part of the overall process of life occurring

simultaneously with other events in the universe and just as important as light exploding off the surface of the sun, the exchange of oxygen and carbon dioxide in the lungs, the earth rotating on its axis, a rain cloud forming, or the synaptic flow of electrical impulses throughout the brain, the raw material of thought and, ultimately, consciousness?

And is it not our most basic fear that this process will stop, for all of us, immediately or slowly, and when it does, we will ultimately have to experience it alone? Is there something transcendent, an existence beyond this purely physical realm? We all hope there is. Many can take comfort in their beliefs. Many of us are willing to endure great physical pain and suffering before giving it up to eternity because we just don't know for certain what, if anything, comes next. And for many of us, the thought of oblivion, of nonexistence, of an end to our consciousness, is more terrifying than the concept of hell. Ultimately, we will all have to experience the one constant, immutable fact of life, which is death.

27

It was the day before New Year's Eve. Turk felt pent-up, and he had to get out of his house, so he decided to go to a basketball game. A small college in the city had developed a program that was able to compete on the national level. He didn't follow sports, but he just didn't want to be alone that evening. He had spent so much time when he wasn't in the office by himself, and his interactions with others in the office were brief and superficial. He would say hi, wish them good morning, ask how things were going, and offer other friendly comments, but that was it. He had no real connection with anyone there. And he had no other relationships. After he got married, his friends from college had slipped away. Everyone was wrapped up in their own lives. Liz and the kids were all he had. Now she was gone and his relationship with his kids was becoming ever more distant.

The arena was small compared to a larger college, but that was its best feature. There wasn't a bad seat in the house, and the students and other fans were passionate and exuberant about their team. The cheerleaders and the college band amplified the excitement. Turk could never understand the attraction by such an overwhelming number of humans to watch spectator sports. He never understood the concept of being a fan. It apparently involved internalizing as a part of one's own identity the exploits of another experienced vicariously. Were their own lives so empty and boring?

Midway through the second half, Turk started to feel anxious. The place was packed with people. Cramped. He felt like he was suffocating. He had a queasy feeling deep in his stomach. He had to get out of there.

He got out of his seat, waded through the others in his aisle, and then walked through the hall at a fast pace to the nearest gate. When he arrived, there was a sign hanging on it that read, "Not an Exit." Turk felt even more claustrophobic. He turned around and felt insignificant in the midst of the crowd of people passing by. Some guy walked past him wearing aviator sunglasses with mirrored lenses. He was wearing sunglasses indoors! Turk could see his reflection in the lenses. Like so many mornings when he did not want to get out of bed and face the day, this had to be like what it felt to be in hell. He could feel the crowd closing in on him. He started walking even faster, almost breaking into a run, until he found the next gate, where he was able to escape into the cold, dark night.

As he walked to his car, he was completely alone. And once he arrived at his house, he would be completely alone. And he would remain alone during New Year's Day and until he went back to work, where he would spend the entire day isolated in his cubicle until he went home that evening to an empty house. He didn't like the crowd or being locked into the stifling prism of their perception of him. But maybe this was worse. Maybe it wasn't others that he feared as much as the absence of other people.

It was two o'clock in the morning, and Turk was still awake. On the stand next to his bed was the latest copy of *The Journal of the American Association of Amateur Psychologists*. He started reading an article about childhood schizophrenia. This guy's theory was that with young people who might be schizophrenic, it was important to intervene early, get them on medication, and try to prevent that big breakdown. Once it happened, there could be permanent brain damage. There could be changes in the physiologic makeup of the brain that could last forever but that could possibly have been prevented.

Turk wondered if maybe something like this had happened to him, not just as a child but throughout his entire life. How had his bad experiences affected him? There was no doubt that his dealings with other people throughout the years, and most recently with Liz and the conflict during the divorce process, had taken a toll, but could he have sustained permanent damage to his brain?

Maybe he had a mental illness. Maybe he always had but didn't know it. Maybe he suspected it was possible, but how could he compare his perception of reality and the inner workings of his mind to that of other people? How could he know whether his thoughts were normal or abnormal? So if he was mentally ill, then it was through the prism of his disease and in this damaged and compromised state that he had lived his entire life and processed everything that he had experienced. Yet even if this was his circumstance, wasn't there hope that he could recover, that he could heal? And wasn't there perhaps also the possibility of grace and redemption?

Turk picked up *The Compendium of the Writings of Felix* and browsed through the pages until he came to a treatise titled "Triumph of the Assclowns: Mediocrity and the Decline of Democracy: The End of Fact-Based or Objective Truth."

Turk didn't have the energy to keep reading. He was now in a place where he felt mentally and physically exhausted enough that he could surrender his waking consciousness to sleep.

28

It was the first Monday of the new year, and Turk was back in his cubicle. In the morning mail he found a memo from Smitty with a check attached in the amount of $80,000 payable to William W. Mahone. The memo stated that the total settlement approved was $100,000 and that a check for $20,000 had been deposited in the administrative expenses fund. Turk was surprised that he had received settlement approval for such a big claim so quickly. The check was dated December 31. Apparently, Smitty wanted this settlement to happen in the previous year. The memo stated that Smitty had approved the settlement and gone ahead and issued the check since Turk was sure that the claimant would accept that amount in full settlement of the claim.

In all his years at American Security, Turk had never heard of the administrative expenses fund. And he had never seen a settlement check issued before the settlement negotiations had been completed. But this only made the process easier and quicker. He wouldn't have to go back to Smitty with another report that he had settled the case within his settlement authority and request that he issue a check. The only step left was to cash it.

Still, this process was unusual, and Turk wanted to be sure Smitty wasn't setting some kind of trap. He went back to the file room and pulled out the hard copy *official* file. In it, he saw that a check in the amount of $20,000 had been issued to "Allen S. Smith, as Trustee for the Administrative Expenses Fund for American Security." The notation in the file read, "Standard 20 percent above total settlement allocated to administrative expenses." This was also something Turk had never seen before. Smitty had apparently instituted some new high-level claims procedure.

Everything looked good, so now it was time for Turk to finish his work of art. As he endorsed the check, he was meticulous in signing the signature of his fictional claimant, William W. Mahone, as sloppily and illegibly as he could to resemble the signature of William V. Malone. One could not distinguish between the *W* and the *V* on the middle initials. The *l* in his last name could easily pass for the sloppy *h* in Mahone. Now Turk had to rely on the hope that the bank teller would not pay enough attention to detail to notice that the name on the check did not exactly match the name on the bank account. On this point, he had to rely on his experience dealing with so many claimants and other humans.

He knew he could count on three of the most predictable and universal traits of human behavior—laziness, incompetence, and lack of attention to detail. These were the constant variables that almost everyone overlooked and failed to factor into the equation. One could take the perfect system, the perfect machine, whatever, but if one interjects the human element, there was always the possibility, perhaps the probability, that something could go wrong. For some inexplicable reason, most people did not take into consideration the incredibly short attention span, the sloppiness, and the almost infinite ability to fuck up of this most noble of primates.

There existed two classes of people—the *fuck-up-ors* and the *fuck-up-ees,* those who made the mistakes and those who were affected. Turk was in both classes. And American Security had made huge profits exploiting human fallibility.

On his way to the bank, Turk pulled into the drive-up lane at a coffee shop and bought a double shot of expresso. This would give him the energy to carry him through the next step on the path to his destiny.

He had been to this branch of the bank many times for his personal business. He always hung back and waited until a window opened up with one of the young female bank tellers. They knew who he was. They knew his name. They would not have their guard up. They would not be suspicious. They would have no reason to scrutinize this transaction; it was just one more of the countless mind-numbing activities that made up their bland day-to-day existence.

Turk had been hiding out so well, deep in the belly of the bell-shaped curve, that he had not drawn attention to himself. He was able to capitalize on his anonymity, his apparent averageness, and the fact that he appeared to be just another disposable widget. He was safe in the middle of the pack, far from the fringes where a predator might target him. So no one suspected him of anything illegal or even unusual. He was one of the mediocre masses.

He dutifully filled out the deposit slip that contained his preprinted account number. As he approached the line, he counted the number of people ahead of him and tried to calculate which teller would finish first and then next, leading to the employee who would conduct this fateful transaction. At that moment, all feeling disappeared from his waist to his feet. He felt only a tingling sensation emanating deep from inside his stomach. He wasn't sure if he was able to walk. The only thing he could do now was keep moving forward, one step at a time, and stick with his plan. *Don't think, don't blink, just keep sleepwalking toward the realization of the grand scheme.* He had already thought it out, planned for every contingency. *Now don't get excited, don't panic, just execute.*

Two people finished their transactions and left, leaving Turk at the front of the line. He would get the next available teller. He had skillfully manipulated his place in line so that Jenny would most likely finish up next. She had processed numerous transactions for him. He knew her name because all the tellers had to wear nametags. He was close enough now that if another window opened up first, he could politely let the person behind him go ahead. He and Jenny were on a first name basis. He could see her counting out the dollar bills. The guy picked up his money and left. Turk was next, and Jenny was his best choice. Turk stepped up to her window. As he did, he faked a limp.

"Hi …" he said, but as he tried to speak, her name sounded like it was stuck in his throat, covered in phlegm. He coughed to clear away the debris. "Hi, Jenny."

"Hello, Mr. Malone," she said. "How can I help you today?"

She remembered his name. That was a good sign.

"Oh, I just need to deposit a check into my account."

Turk handed Jenny the check with the deposit slip on top. She began punching keys on her machine and then picked up the check.

Jenny was so young. She had to be barely out of high school. She had pimples that she covered up with makeup, just like his fast-food Madonna. She had a roll of baby fat around her otherwise attractive figure.

He wondered if she had been among the class of students who, even in high school, were somehow destined to take boring jobs not for the short-term but permanently and live mediocre, bland, and boring lives, at least while at work, which sucked up the majority of people's time. Being a claims adjuster was bad enough, but if he had to do various other jobs like being a bank teller, working on an assembly line, waiting tables, operating a cash register, or being a janitor, he did not think he could handle it.

She punched a couple more keys with her right hand. She was still holding the check with her left hand. Wasn't she now supposed to place it in the slot next to her machine? Shouldn't he be starting to hear the sound of his receipt being printed? She seemed to be studying it. Had she noticed something? Why was this taking so long?

"Looks like someone hit the lottery," she said finally.

Turk froze. These people must be specially trained. He knew this was the riskiest part of his scheme. His knees locked, and he still had no feeling in his legs, only a queasy feeling deep in his bowels. In a flash, he could see his entire life unraveling. They would take him to jail. They would charge him with a felony. He would have to come up with enough money to post a bond or stay in jail. Liz would not help him. He'd lose his job. And this was even before he went to trial. Then he most certainly would be found guilty.

Once convicted, he would be sent to prison, where he would have no protection. He would become somebody's bitch. Some brutal convict would fuck him in the ass at will. He would probably test positive for HIV and have to be on a combination of medications for the rest of his life. He would exist in a deeper realm of hell than he was already experiencing.

He wasn't sure, but he thought a fart might have slipped out amid the general numbness, squeaking out between his butt cheeks, but he didn't hear it. He hoped Jenny couldn't hear it either. He sniffed, and there was no foul smell. As he started to respond, it sounded to him like he was speaking into a long tunnel.

"Pardon me?" he said finally.

"I said it looks like someone has hit the lottery."

Turk's diaphragm suddenly released, resulting in an awkward chuckle that resembled the quacking of a duck. "Oh yes. Well, no," responded Turk. He realized he was talking too loudly. He lowered his voice. "I broke my ankle in an accident, but it's okay now. It was the other guy's fault, so the insurance company gave me a settlement to compensate me for my injury."

Turk could hear the reassuring sound of his deposit receipt printing. It was almost over now. He would wait a couple of days for the check to clear, and the money would be his, free and clear. Jenny handed him the receipt.

"Thank you. Have a good day now," she said.

"I most certainly will, and thank you," Turk said.

Jenny laughed. It was not a sincere, spontaneous reaction as if Turk had just said something witty or engaged her in a bit of Oscar Wildian repartee, but the type of forced polite chuckle used to end a conversation.

The muscles in Turk's body loosened with each step he took toward the exit. He continued to fake the limp. The numbness in his legs started to wear off. He stepped out into a cold but sunny January day. In the middle of winter, a day like this was a gift. There were no leaves on the trees, and along the streets and parking lots, snow was piled up, not clear and white but covered with dark residue from the exhausts of cars and buses. But the sky was a clear and deep blue. Huge cumulus clouds floated in the air like ephemeral fortresses.

Sprawling before Turk were vast expanses of asphalt covering what had once been fields or farmland—one parking lot connected to an access road that connected to another parking lot that surrounded a strip mall, and then another parking lot that surrounded yet another strip mall with restaurants, stores, and gas stations interspersed.

Turk had done it! This was his new beginning. For the first time in a long while, at least since college, at least since those waning years of his youth when everything seemed possible, when the operative word was *potential*, he felt truly alive!

On the periphery of his vision, he caught a glimpse of several angels emerging from one of the huge cumulus clouds and then quickly disappearing into another. He had been functioning on so little sleep for so long, was it possible that this was a dream breaking through into his waking life? No, absolutely not. This was no doubt a fissure, an overlap, in parallel dimensions. And Turk was a witness.

29

The next day, before he left for work, Turk sent an email to Abdullah, inquiring about the status of locating the chimps. By midmorning, Turk's default mode of fear and anxiety had kicked in. He started second-guessing himself and his actions. Was there some minor detail that he had overlooked that could lead to the discovery of his crime? He was a big-picture guy, after all. Once he pulled off the PPP, he would be able to let others tend to the details.

He had read numerous self-help books that talked about the need to think positively, eliminate negative thoughts, and attract the things that you want into your life. But that advice wasn't written for criminals.

Throughout the rest of the day, he kept replaying in his mind the steps he had taken to carry out his fraud and whether something that he had done or failed to do might have left a clue. As he drove home, his thoughts were swirling uncontrollably. He was overwhelmed, almost immobilized. He had trouble driving his car and focusing on the road.

When he arrived home that evening, he logged onto his computer, and there it was—a response from Mr. Abdullah.

Mr. Malone:

I have located a group of seven chimpanzees. Although you requested twelve, despite our best efforts, we could only locate seven. Because of circumstances beyond our control, the price has fluctuated. Although we had quoted you an estimated $60,000 to $70,000 for twelve chimps, we can now only provide you with seven chimps at a price of $80,000. This includes our fees in finding the chimps, packing and shipping costs, and other miscellaneous fees. After subtracting the $10,000 you have already paid, your total remaining cost will be $70,000.

If you are agreeable to these terms, we can have the chimps shipped to you within a week. Please respond as soon as possible, as this offer will only remain open for seven days. If you agree, I will send you instructions on where to meet us to pick up the chimpanzees. Since you have requested that all transactions be carried out in cash, we expect that you will arrive at the port of destination with $70,000 in cash.

Respectfully,
Jaleel Abdullah

Turk knew that he had gotten screwed again. But at least he had seen it coming, maybe. He had known who he was dealing with. He had known he couldn't trust them. But it could have been worse. They could have simply taken the $10,000 down payment and never followed up to provide the chimps. Actually, seven would be an easier number to manage than twelve. But when one cuts the number almost in half, the price of $80,000 was not much more competitive than the original quote he had obtained before going on the black market. But this was where he was. Abdullah had the chimps, which he could deliver soon, and Turk would have the cash. He typed in his response.

> Mr. Abdullah,
>
> I must say that I am disappointed that you did not keep your word and are now requesting essentially the same amount of money that you had quoted me but for only half the number of chimps that I had requested. Nonetheless, I accept your offer. I can make myself available within the next week to complete the transaction. Please send me the instructions on when and where to meet you to pick up the chimps. I will be there with $70,000 United States dollars.

The next evening as he waited to hear back from Abdullah, he went to Big Ray's Superstore, where he knew he could purchase all the items he needed to finish his preparations for the basement, where he would house his chimps. At the entrance to the store was a life-size image of Big Ray. A huge picture of his entire body had been cut out and plastered to a giant piece of cardboard that had also been cut out to conform to the shape of his giant frame. He was a big man, at least six feet seven inches tall and probably about three hundred pounds. He had a huge grin on his face. Turk walked up to the cardboard Big Ray, put his face directly in Big Ray's face, and looked Big Ray straight in the eye.

Turk went first to the Music Center and purchased several CDs of classical music. His plan was to blast the most beautiful music of the ages into the basement. And of course, occasionally he would sneak in a little Felix. This would help to unconsciously open the chimpanzee minds to the higher concepts Turk was going to teach them. He also purchased a *Beginning Piano* book.

He went next to the Pet Center and picked up seven extra-large bags of dog food. He knew this was not their natural diet, but it would have to do for now. He also bought seven extra-large bags of cat litter. He had already purchased three huge troughs that were in the basement, one for water, one for dog food, and one for cat litter. He doubted the chimps would confine their shitting and pissing to this one trough filled with cat litter, but if it worked, it would make his cleanup efforts much easier.

He then went to the Produce Center and bought a crate of bananas.

His next stop was the Book Center, where he picked up a book on sign language. This was how he would open the lines of communication with his animal cousins.

He went next to the Sports Center. Initially, he intended to buy a handgun for protection but decided they were too expensive and didn't really address his anticipated need for protection from the chimps. He would be in close quarters with them, and if he felt threatened, he would not want to kill these animals that he had purchased at such a high price and who were the raw material of his dream.

He decided his best course of action would be to buy a knife that he could carry on his waist and whip out, if necessary, at any moment. He decided he would also buy a staple gun at the Hardware Center. Those suckers were so powerful that they could injure and even maim someone, or some chimp, if not used for their intended purpose. And if threatened, he did not intend to use it for its intended purpose. He also decided to buy pepper spray that he could spray into their eyes if necessary, although he wasn't sure it would work on such large beasts.

Of course, the problem with any of these methods of protection was that he would be down in the basement alone with seven chimps and that each one would be seven times stronger than him and so physically superior and quicker that they could neutralize him at any moment. He didn't have the luxury of keeping his distance, bearing down on them through the sights of a rifle, and pulling the trigger.

Turk went next to the Electronics Center, where he bought a webcam that he planned to install on the ceiling of the basement so he could monitor the chimps from his home office on the first floor. He also bought a pair of speakers that he could hook into his CD player to blast the classical music into the basement.

He then went to the Hardware Center, where he purchased the staple gun and also a dead bolt lock that he would install on the basement door. The primates he was planning to develop could easily figure out how to turn a handle and open a door. He would need more protection.

His last stop was the Photo Center. He had printed two pictures off the internet. He blew them up to poster size. One was a photo of Ham, who was the first chimp in outer space, the first chimponaut. The other was a painting of Hanuman, the Hindu monkey god. He had a monkey's face on a muscular human body and a long tail looped over his shoulder.

He had to bow to Big Ray. This place was great. It had everything. There was no need to go to numerous different stores. One could find it all right here. Big Ray had not only found a need but many needs and had filled not just a need but many needs. He was truly a visionary. He wasn't only ahead of his time; he was able to implement his vision in real time, this time, right now.

When Turk arrived at home that evening, he immediately logged onto his computer. The instructions from Abdullah had arrived. They would meet at midnight in only two days. Abdullah provided specific instructions on how to get to a small pier, where they would meet at a remote, isolated location on one of the Great Lakes.

Turk went down into the basement and installed the webcam and the speakers. Then he fitted the dead bolt lock onto the basement door. He filled the respective troughs with dog food, water, and cat litter. He hung the pictures of Ham and Hanuman next to each other in a corner of the basement and placed a rug on the floor beneath them. Everything was in place. This was actually happening! When he returned with the chimps, he would open the door to the basement and lead them into the beginning of a new reality that only he could envision.

Later that evening he went to bed, and as usual, he could not fall asleep. He pulled an article out of his stack of materials and began reading about a Ugandan village that had been repeatedly raided by a pack of chimpanzees. Because of the clearing of the jungle to create farmland, the chimps had been steadily losing their habitat and, in search of food, were destroying crops and terrorizing this small community close to the edge of the forest. Then one day, the villagers were horrified when a large chimp snatched a toddler, ran back into the forest, and killed him.

Turk was also horrified by what he had just read. He put the article down. This story was not helping him get drowsy. It only got him further aroused. He picked up his remote and started clicking wildly, jumping from channel to channel. He stopped when he came to the *Real Animals* program on cable television. And there it was. Turk knew it could happen someday.

> "This was a historic moment. This was the first time that anyone had ever witnessed a chimpanzee, with what appeared to be malice forethought, and not even in self-defense, use a tool as a weapon against another chimp. Until now, it was believed that using tools to inflict pain, suffering, and death was something that only humans did …"

The researchers studying the pack had named the chimp Imoso. A huge image of the beast flashed onto the television screen. He was snarling with his mouth wide open, revealing huge sharp incisors. What was even more startling was the fact that he had inflicted this abuse upon his mate. He was a simian wifebeater!

The next morning, functioning on little sleep and high doses of caffeine, Turk had to continue with his job duties. He planned to leave the next day, which was Thursday, for the rendezvous with Abdullah and the chimps. As soon as he arrived in the office, he sent a vacation request to Smitty for two vacation days. He would have a four-day weekend to complete the mission that he hoped would free him from his day-to-day drudgery and possibly make him rich someday. Smitty, always timely and efficient, responded within fourteen minutes and approved the request, although he reminded Turk that, per office policy, vacation requests were to be submitted at least two months in advance. He wrote in his email that he would make an exception for Turk because of his "lengthy tenure and loyalty to American Security and its subsidiaries."

Turk had scheduled an appointment later that morning to take a statement from a claimant on a slip-and-fall case. She had fallen on a sidewalk and injured her knee. Every time he drove into this part of the city, he felt a sense of impending disaster. Although he would be picking up his chimps tomorrow night, he had to keep doing his job and keep up appearances.

He was entering the decaying area of the city where he was born. His family had moved out when he was just seven years old, so he had only vague memories of his childhood here. It had been a nicer neighborhood back then. The small aluminum-sided houses all looked the same, but back then they had been new and well-maintained. Almost every family had children, so there were kids everywhere. It appeared that every time one of these families saved enough money to buy a nicer home, they moved to the suburbs and the city kept expanding outward, leaving the center to deteriorate like a dying star collapsing in on itself and creating a giant black hole.

At the end of the block was a cemetery. Turk had vivid memories of it. He had not liked living near a place where so many dead bodies were buried. There was a chemical plant nearby and next to that another factory surrounded by giant propane tanks. The entire area was permeated with a foul manufactured smell that resembled a mixture of human excrement and disinfectant, and Turk always worried that one of the enormous tanks could blow at any moment, taking out the entire neighborhood, killing not only the living but also obliterating the remains of the corpses buried in the cemetery, killing these dead people yet a second time in a lake of fire.

Turk felt that something unnatural, something out of order with the elemental rhythms of life and the universe, perhaps something evil, emanated from this place. Maybe these homes and streets should never have been built here. The entire place was deteriorating. Maybe it should be left alone to decay. It was as if he were trespassing on a sacred Native American burial ground.

Or maybe he had unconsciously channeled into the collective consciousness and was experiencing what it would have been like to walk into the center of Hiroshima just before the atomic blast. He felt he could sense the collective force of all those souls about to be annihilated in one irrevocable instant. Was that one unimaginable eruption of energy enough not only to kill them but also to wipe out their souls, blot them out completely, leaving no trace that they had ever existed? Turk wondered what type of shock wave the deaths of all those people and the possible obliteration of all their souls in one moment may have sent throughout the universe. Was it still reverberating out there, traveling endlessly into infinity?

He was now deep into the dying neighborhood. He could sense the earth trembling beneath him. Perhaps an earthquake was about to erupt. Perhaps something cataclysmic was forming. Maybe the immutable laws of nature were changing. Perhaps the speed of light was accelerating, a cosmic change, a variance in the invariable.

After the appointment, he went back to his house. After all the time and energy spent getting the money into his checking account, he realized that he had not put any thought into how to get the cash out of his account. He knew banks were required to report to the federal government any withdrawals of $10,000 or more. So would that send up a red flag?

He did as he had done so often before and conducted an online search. He found an article that laid out a strategy to withdraw the money and hopefully not set off any alarms. It was his money, after all. The purpose behind the law was to help detect money laundering schemes—transactions designed to take cash received in drug deals and other illegal activity and "launder" it so it could be used in legitimate commerce. The author of the article advised that one should simply meet with the banker to describe why the money was being withdrawn and demonstrate that it was for a legal, legitimate purpose.

It was now midafternoon. As Turk drove to the bank, he concocted a scenario that he thought might work. When he entered, there was no line, and Jenny was at the teller window.

"Hi, Jenny. I need to make a large withdrawal. Can I talk to one of the branch managers?"

"Sure," she responded with a huge smile. She was good. He felt like she was genuinely glad to see him, although intellectually, he knew that it could not be true. "Let me see if he is available."

She went back to the offices. After less than a minute, she returned and led him back to the manager's office. The manager stood up, and they shook hands. Turk sat down across the desk from him.

"The reason I wanted to meet with you," said Turk, "is that I would like to withdraw $70,000 in cash from my checking account. I know that this will be reported to the federal government and that the withdrawal of such a large amount could raise suspicions. I read an article that said that since I have a legitimate purpose for wanting to withdraw the money in cash, my money, that I should meet with my banker and explain the reason for the withdrawal. So I don't know how this works, and I'm not sure if it even matters to you. I'm just following the advice in the article."

"Yes, that's fine," the manager said.

"I'm not planning to use this money for any nefarious purpose. The reason I need to withdraw this money in cash is that I'm involved with a ministry in my church, and we have a sister parish in Nigeria. We are planning a mission trip there next month to provide medical care and, more importantly, to start construction of a medical clinic. We have conducted many missionary missions to our sister parish in the past and have found that, because of corruption and bureaucratic red tape, it is much easier to do the Lord's work on a cash-only basis."

"Okay, I understand," said the manager. "I will make a note of our conversation and put in the file. You can have Jenny withdraw the cash for you."

"Oh, thank you very much," said Turk. "And I thank you not only for myself but also on behalf of our church and especially the members of our sister parish."

"My pleasure," he responded. "And good luck with your magnanimous endeavor."

As Turk walked out of the bank with the cash, he was a little surprised at what a good liar he had become. He was able to pull it off because it was in support of a truly noble cause, the PPP.

30

Two days later, he was approaching the appointed place at the appointed time. He had been driving for hours. It had been interstate most of the way. It took him to the edge of this godforsaken industrial wasteland located on the southern shore of one of the Great Lakes. The exit ramp had deposited him at the outskirts of this forbidden zone. According to Abdullah's directions, Turk was to continue directly north. His ultimate destination was an isolated dock where he would take delivery of his revolutionary cargo and begin the final phase of the fulfillment of his destiny.

He was driving a large rental van with a cargo box on the back like the ones he had rented when he was in college and moving his possessions from his dorm room to his home or an apartment off campus. It was a mild night for mid-January. It had rained, and the air was moist. Fog rose off the pavement. Even though the air in the cab had been cycled through the heater, it still smelled foul and unnatural.

He had kept driving. In the distance were chemical and manufacturing plants, huge smokestacks, elaborate arrays of pipelike fixtures, and massive storage tanks. Just like the neighborhood where he was born, he felt like the entire place could explode at any moment. This was no place for candles, but on top of one of the factories was a perpetual bluish flame.

A number of small cities had grown up throughout this area, wedged between the giant factories. Each was a separate municipality. The entire atmosphere of the place had to be unhealthy. There were probably pockets of mutants spread around the region. A lot of shit had gone down here. A lot of people had made a lot of money rearranging the basic elements of life to create products that generated huge profits, and he had to admit, they had either found or created a need and then fulfilled that need. Was this the inevitable result of his core belief when taken to its logical conclusion?

He drove past a vast pit that appeared to be filled with industrial sludge. Steam was rising from the muck. It appeared that something could be brewing in the depths of that giant hole, that something was forming, something terrifying and deformed, maybe some new life-form, a precursor of the beasts that would come near the end of time. He could state that he had been here and stared deep into the bowels of re-creation, the modern synthetic equivalent to the primordial bog from which life first arose.

He was driving through a dimension where industry and manufacturing were transforming the physical universe in a way that was profit-driven, soulless, and godless. He pulled the truck over to the edge of the road. His job was not to make judgments but to bear witness. He had his hammer and chisel with him, as he always did. Between the side of the road and the edge of the pit was a sign that read, "Hauling of Radioactive Materials by Special Permit Only." It was mounted in a large base of cement. Turk had become proficient at this task. It only took a few minutes. It would last. He etched it in clean and deep—*Turk*.

He finally arrived at a long, narrow pier. This was where he was to meet Abdullah and take possession of the noble primates. His instructions said he was to turn off his headlights as soon as he reached the entrance to the pier. He complied, but this made it even more difficult to see into the darkness ahead.

Near the end of the pier, a neon sign stood out high in the night. It read simply, Gas. He parked the truck and got out. In contrast to the artificial light, the darkness beyond seemed endless and unfathomable, as if there were no light out there.

He suddenly became afraid. He looked back at the bright sign. As he stared directly into the artificial light, he thought he could feel the pupils of his eyes contract into microscopic peepholes. He feared that his eye muscles might get stuck and he could be blinded. He stared back into the darkness. He thought he could feel his pupils dilate to the point that they consumed the entire irises in both eyes. He feared the force of gravity in the deep darkness beyond could rip his soul and his conscious being right out of his body and into the vast, infinite blackness, like a celestial body, suspended in space, being drawn ever faster, with no possibility of escape, even faster than the speed of light, into a collapsing star.

He realized he had to get a grip on his emotions. He was at a crossroads now. This was no time to panic. He walked past the neon sign, deeper into the night, and shined his flashlight outward. He could see no stars overhead.

He thought he sensed motion emerging from the darkness. He turned off the flashlight so that he would not stand out in the total blackness that surrounded him. God, he hoped it was Abdullah and not some predator. Turk was exposed. He had no weapons. He had no way to defend himself against any criminals or gangs or wild dogs. He wasn't even sure that something was out there. Perhaps he had detected this from some combination of his smell and hearing. He couldn't see anything, but he thought he felt something. Perhaps he was receiving a signal emanating from deep inside the reptilian part of his brain firing haphazardly through the remnants of ancient neurocircuitry that had atrophied ages ago over thousands of years of evolution.

Then a huge set of white teeth glimmered directly in front of his face. He could see the whites of a pair of bloodshot eyes. It was

Abdullah. Turk flipped on his flashlight, and shined it directly into Abdullah's face. He wore a huge grin.

"Good evening, Mr. Malone. It is nice to see you again."

"Hello, Mr. Abdullah. I'm certainly glad to see you, or anyone for that matter," Turk said.

"You will be pleased to know that the shipment has arrived as planned."

"Excellent," said Turk.

"Give me the money and wait here," said Abdullah. "These are delicate matters. It's best for you that you not meet these men face-to-face. You should keep as much distance as you can."

Turk walked back to the truck and opened the passenger door to the cab. He opened the glove compartment and took out a plastic bag containing the $70,000 in cash. He walked back to Abdullah.

"Turn the truck around and back it up to entrance to the pier, just past the neon sign," said Abdullah. "And wait for me. I'll be back soon."

There was no way Turk would give him the money and watch him disappear into the darkness trusting that he would return with the chimps.

"Sorry, Mr. Abdullah," he said. "Don't be offended, but I will not turn over the $70,000 until I have my chimps."

"I understand," said Abdullah. "We have not spent enough time together for me to have built your trust. You keep the money for now. Go ahead and turn your truck around and back it up. Watch me in your rearview mirrors, and I will guide you to the edge of the pier."

Turk rolled down the driver's side window as he had been instructed. Abdullah guided him to the edge of the pier and then held up his hands for Turk to stop.

Turk could hear Abdullah open the back door to the cargo compartment. He looked in the mirror on the passenger's side of the vehicle and saw Abdullah walk back into the darkness. As he stared, he focused his gaze on the blackness where he thought the night sky and the Great Lake came together on the horizon, where two infinities merged. He saw several shadowy figures carrying crates into the back of the van. He could feel it bounce up and down as the chimps were loaded. He knew there was some type of ship docked back there on the water, but it had no lights on, and he could not make out any details. Abdullah appeared to his left just outside the open window to the cab.

"The chimpanzees have been loaded into the back of the van," he said. "Would you like to inspect them before you turn over the money and complete the transaction?"

"Yes, absolutely," said Turk.

He got out of the cab and went to the back of the van. Abdullah raised the back door. Turk pointed his flashlight inside, and there were seven chimpanzees, each in a separate crate made of plywood. The boards were placed several inches apart, apparently to allow in air. He could see his chimps through those spaces. A hairy paw stuck out from one of the crates. In another was a much smaller chimp, a baby chimp.

Turk felt a surge of energy swell up from deep inside his being. He was so close now. Years from now, humanoid kind would look back on this as a historic moment. Everything was falling into place as it was, as it should have been, and as it would forever be. All Turk had to do now was take care of his monkeys! Turk gave the plastic bag containing the $70,000 to Abdullah.

"I'll wait while you count the money," said Turk.

As he had done before, he had wrapped the one-hundred-dollar bills into bundles of ten and wrapped them together with rubber bands.

Abdullah opened the bag and looked inside.

"I can see seven packets," he said. "There is no need for me to examine any further. I know that you are a man of your word. Go in peace, my brother, and good luck on your new endeavor. Maybe someday our paths will cross again. Now get in the cab and drive. And for your own protection, don't look back. The less you know, the less you heard, the less you saw, the better. Do not stop until you have reached your final destination. And do not exceed the speed limit. It is important for your sake and ours that you do not arouse any suspicion. You have probably heard the saying, 'If you are going to break the big rules, don't break the little ones.'"

Turk, of course, having been told not to look back, did just that. The faint glow of the taillights illuminated Abdullah's form, and then he disappeared into the darkness.

Turk pressed the accelerator to the floor, and the truck shot forward. He heard a rumbling sound and the truck bounced as the cargo behind him apparently shifted backward.

He drove back through the labyrinth of factories and cesspools. He drove just as he had been instructed. He did not falter. He did not waiver. Finally, he reached the interstate. As he cruised up the entrance ramp, he felt safer. He had reached the anonymous stream of commerce. He could easily blend in. And it would deliver him to within a few miles of his house.

He continued to drive. He wanted to stop and examine his new tribe of primates, but he would wait. Abdullah was right. He shouldn't risk drawing any suspicion. He drove the exact speed limit. He stayed in the right lane and was careful to stay in the middle of his lane. He kept driving. He could see only the lines on the pavement and the road ahead of him up to where the glare from the headlights ended. Beyond and on all sides was darkness broken only by the occasional set of headlights coming toward him from the opposite direction. He knew the way back. There was no need to think. At some point, his mind detached and drifted off, and his body was driving the van on autopilot.

After a couple of hours, he really had to piss. Sure, Abdullah had said not to stop. But Turk could get away with this one minor deviation from the plan. It was dark and deserted at this time in the morning. He wouldn't even get off the highway. It was his bladder, after all.

He slowed the van and pulled onto the right side of the road until it was completely off the highway. He left the motor running and jumped out of the cab, leaving the door open. He crossed in front of the truck and stepped first onto an area where he could feel that the pavement under his feet was deteriorating and breaking up into large chunks, then onto a strip of gravel. On the other side was a steep slope. Because of the darkness, he couldn't tell how far down it went or how sharp the angle was. Had he pulled the truck too far off the highway, it could have been disaster. Although it was probably only about ten to fifteen feet down, it surely would have caused the truck to flip. Turk stood on the edge, whipped out his penis, and began pissing into the deep, dark abyss.

As he climbed back into the cab, he heard a rustling sound in the back. Should he sneak a peek? Abdullah had said not to stop. But after this much drive time, checking his cargo would be the prudent thing to do. He grabbed his flashlight and darted to the back of the truck. He popped the latch and raised the door about six inches so he could peer underneath. He shined his flashlight inside and could see numerous pairs of eyes staring back at him. He heard a shuffling sound to his right. When he looked, a monkey paw protruded out from underneath the door. He quickly closed the door onto the chimp's wrist to keep it from extending its arm farther out. He was careful not to press too hard and injure the beast. The hairy hand withdrew, and Turk was able to close the door and latch the lock.

Had one of his newly owned primates escaped from its crate? It was now urgent that he complete his mission as soon as possible and get the chimps delivered safely into his basement. Turk ran back to the cab, jumped in, and gunned the accelerator.

After he had traveled a few miles, he heard a loud thump against the wall behind his seat and could feel the vibration. He heard two loud thumps against the back door. He could hear other noises that sounded like rumbling and chaos and finally a loud slapping sound as something butted up against the side of the cargo area. He could feel the entire back of the van rock from side to side. What was going on back there? Were these beasts trying to escape?

After another five to ten miles, the activity in the back subsided. It was less than half an hour to his house, but he was operating on pure adrenaline. He knew he shouldn't risk stopping again, but he needed more fuel. He needed caffeine and sugar.

It was still completely dark. He pulled off the interstate into a gas station and purchased a large cup of coffee to which he added cream and three packets of sugar. He also grabbed a donut, which he popped into his mouth as he exited the station. He had only lost a few minutes and soon was back on the road. He started chugging the cup of coffee like it was a glass of whiskey. He had to hang on. He had to concentrate on completing the next step, get the chimps to his house, and finish his trip. He reached over into his backpack and pulled out the CDs he had brought with him for the trip. These might help him get through this final stretch.

Don't Eat the Donut, Eat the Hole: Losing Weight Is Just a State of Mind
So Be It Now—No, Even Sooner
Practice Dying: A Primer
The Mathematician's Guide to Eternity: Infinity plus infinity equals infinity; infinity times infinity equals infinity; infinity times divinity equals _____?

None of these would work. He couldn't focus on anything but his chimps. As he neared his house with his prized cargo, he should have felt a moment of victory and pure exhilaration. Instead, he felt like he was a surfer riding a giant wave that could collapse in on him at any moment. He turned on the radio. Commercials were playing.

"It ain't so ea-sy when you're O-C-D—see! Ask your doctor about our newest serotonin reuptake inhibitor, the most advanced treatment for

depression and obsessive-compulsive disorder. *It's your life, live it, don't double-check it!* We can help."

"Zitgeist—the Zeitgeist in Acne Care ..."

Finally, he arrived at the interstate exit nearest his house. Ten minutes later, he was at his driveway. He backed up the van as he opened the garage door with the remote control. He parked within a couple of feet of the opening. This was where it would get difficult. His original plan had been to unload each chimp, still in its crate, from the truck and into the garage, close the garage door, and then take each one down the stairs into the basement. It wasn't until he had transported all the chimps into the basement that he had planned to decide when and in what manner he would release them from their crates. But the possibility that one of the chimps had escaped from its crate made this plan unworkable. As he walked from the cab to the back of the van, he could hear the chimps rumbling and making guttural noises. The intensity was increasing.

Turk realized that the first thing he was going to have to deal with was the rebellious troublemaker who appeared to have escaped from his crate. He went to the kitchen and returned to the garage with a bunch of bananas. His hope was that the chimp would not be combative and that he could use the bananas to lure the rogue chimp into the basement. With the garage door open, he knew there was a risk that the chimp could escape, but he had no choice other than to accept this risk. There was also a risk that the chimp would be combative. Turk picked up the baseball bat in the corner of the garage. This was the only method he could think of to mitigate that potential threat. He did not want to injure or kill the beast. He had paid good money for him, after all, and he would be instrumental in the realization of Turk's dream. But like all forms of life on this planet, Turk's first priority was to protect himself.

He unlatched the lock and raised the back door about a foot high. A foul smell hit him full in the face—a mixture of shit, piss, and sweat infused with dirty and matted animal hair. The odor entered through his nostrils and permeated his sinuses. He felt a slight stinging sensation in his forehead. Again, he could see pairs of eyes staring back at him through the openings in the crates. In the closest crate, Turk could see a small chimp, a baby chimp. Mucous ran from its nose, and there was a green clot in the corner of its eye. It looked up at Turk, and as he looked into its eyes, he thought the baby chimp looked sad. Of course, Turk had no way of knowing, but he felt a connection.

Suddenly, the rogue chimp lunged against the trailer door, hitting it hard and then falling back. He tried to squeeze through the opening but couldn't do it, except for his paws and forearms. Turk slammed the van door onto the rogue chimp's forearms. The chimp quickly withdrew his paws back into the truck.

So what was Turk's next move? He realized he had not prepared well for this moment. All he had ever focused on was the chimps' potential humanity, not that they were actually wild animals. He had not thought much about his own self-protection in the midst of these primitive beings as he tried to take them to the next level.

This was the turning point. He had been building up to this moment since he first conceived of the PPP. His only option now was to neutralize this chimp. He was the only thing standing in Turk's way. And as he did so, all the chimps would be watching from inside their crates. Once he deposed their leader and made him subservient, the rest of the chimps would follow suit. Turk would be the leader, the alpha male. He would be in control. All he needed to do now was summon up the courage. If necessary, he would engage in hand-to-paw combat. But he had an advantage. Like the human he was, he had a weapon—his baseball bat. He would take the chimp head-on!

He pulled up the back door to the van and thrust it all the way to the top. The primate stood up on his hind legs about three feet from Turk and hissed at him. Then it fell quiet. His chimpanzee penis was at Turk's eye level, directly in his face. Behind the chimp, Turk could see six pairs of eyes staring at him through the openings in the crates. He could not read the rogue chimp's body language or facial expression. Was he going to attack? Turk looked the beast directly in the eyes. This was no time to show fear. He dared not make any sudden movements that could provoke the creature. He might be willing to fight to the death if necessary. And Turk did not want to kill him, only subdue him. The chimp hissed again.

Turk lunged forward and swung his bat at the chimp, aiming for his rib cage. The chimp pivoted, and the bat struck him on his right upper arm. The beast lunged from the van, hit Turk in the chest, and knocked him backward. The bat flew out of his hand. He fell onto his back on the concrete floor. The chimp jumped on top of him and seized his throat with its right paw. Turk felt an intense stabbing pain as the chimp's sharp claws ripped into the flesh around his neck. He couldn't breathe. With both hands, he grabbed the animal's forearm. He used his left hand to try to pry its fingers away, but the claws dug in deeper. Blood oozed onto the concrete. Turk could not free his throat from the vicelike grip. He was starting to fade. Was this how he was going to go out?

From some visceral place deep within, the thought started to build in his mind: *Bite the monkey! Bite the monkey!* He had teeth. He placed his left hand on the chimp's right forearm and with his right hand reached across his opponent's right upper arm. With all his strength, Turk started bending the chimp's arm at the elbow, pulling its face close to his. He looked directly into the eyes of the beast, deep, dark, unfathomable. Turk had a clear opening to strike at the chimp's throat.

In that instant, Turk opened his jaws and lunged upward. He connected with animal's throat and sunk his teeth in deep. It was a clean shot. The chimp's paw loosened from around Turk's neck, leaving deep gashes. Blood continued to pour from his wounds. The creature collapsed onto him. He kept his jaw tight and his teeth firmly planted on the chimp's jugular. He grabbed the chimp's back and rolled him over so that he was on top, biting down on the chimp's neck. Turk had him now. He was in control. The chimp started to squirm, but Turk sunk his teeth in even farther. For good measure, he rammed his knee into the chimp's balls. If Turk squeezed his jaws any tighter, this would be the death bite.

As he thought about his next move, the beast went limp. Turk couldn't believe what had just happened. The rogue chimp had surrendered. Turk had won! He released his jaws from the chimp's neck and rose to his knees. He had huge chunks of the chimp's fur in both hands, which he had ripped off the chimp's back. Turk had bled onto the chimp, and his blood had mixed into its fur. He immediately took off his blood-soaked shirt and wrapped it around his own neck to stop the bleeding.

He placed his arms underneath the limp frame of the beast and lifted it off the pavement. Turk stood and turned to face the rest of the pack. The chimps stared at him in silence. He raised the limp body of the former primate king, their deposed leader, over his head. He was surprised at how thin and emaciated the chimp was. Turk made a huge, almost snarling grin and tried to mimic the same smug expression that he had seen so many times on Smitty's face. He felt a sense of adrenaline-induced ecstasy. He had triumphed. Finally, he was the head of the pack!

Once he had subdued their leader, the only task left was to get the chimps into the basement. He carried down their leader first and laid him on the cold concrete floor. Then he hauled each crate down separately. This was difficult because the chimps were heavy, so he had to walk backward, pulling the crates from behind, dragging them on the concrete floor of the garage and then across the kitchen floor, leaving several gashes, to the edge of the basement steps. Then he had to slide the huge animals down the steps to the basement floor.

One of the chimps was missing an eye. The eyelid was closed and surrounded by scar tissue. It appeared to have been clawed out in a fight with another chimp. All the chimps were males. There would be no possibility of procreation among the pack. This was probably done deliberately by the Nigerians. If he wanted to increase the size of the pack, he would have to go back to them to purchase female chimps.

He was so exhausted at that point that he left the chimps in their crates. He would free them after he had gotten some sleep. He climbed slowly back up the basement steps and locked the deadbolt behind him. He went to the garage, backed the van into it, and hit the button to close the garage door.

31

When Turk woke up, he did not know how long it had been. Although he had set the alarm, he must have been in such a deep sleep that he turned it off without waking up. He could have been asleep for seven hours or seven days. He had no idea. He could only hope that nothing bad had happened to the chimps as they languished in the basement during his extended period of unconsciousness. He dressed quickly. He had to let them out of their crates as soon as possible so that they could access the dog food and water that he had set out for them. He logged onto his computer, but when he clicked on the icon for the videocam he had set up in the basement, there was no picture.

He went to the basement door so he could descend just far enough to see the entire basement and assess the situation. He walked down several steps. The foul stench hit him full in the face. The chimps were scurrying around. They had busted out of their crates, and plywood was scattered throughout the entire basement. The webcam had been ripped off the ceiling and lay on the floor. The troughs with water and dog food were almost empty. They had not defecated into the trough filled with cat litter. Shit was everywhere. They obviously had already taken care of their basic needs. So Turk's most urgent concern had been addressed by the chimps on their own initiative.

Turk descended one more step. The acrid scent of ammonia made his eyes water. The chimps ceased their activities and stared up at him. He felt more like an intruder than their leader. He was afraid to go down and walk alone among them, not without more protection. He quickly withdrew from the basement, closed the door, and locked the deadbolt.

Before making his first, hopefully triumphal, descent into the basement, he had to clean and return the rental van. Despite the fact it was January, he hosed down the back, flushing the chimp turds onto the driveway and into the grass. He dropped off the van and picked up his car, which he had left at the rental store. On the way back to his house, he stopped at the local Boy Scout headquarters and picked up uniforms for the chimps. He bought seven extra-large Boy Scout shirts for him and the six grown-up chimps and a Cub Scout shirt for the baby chimp.

After he arrived at his house, he starting planning his first entrance into his minikingdom. Although he had defeated their leader, this did not necessarily guarantee that he would be safe with all the chimps having been released from their crates. He had learned from his first battle with the now deposed chimp leader that a baseball bat did not provide sufficient protection. But he was surprised that he had been able to bend the arm of the chimp leader to bring him face-to-face with him, even though Turk had used both of his arms against only the chimp's right arm. He also didn't understand why, when he grabbed the chimp's back to pull the beast off his body, so much of the chimp's fur ripped off into his hands.

He changed into his Boy Scout shirt and went into the garage. Along with his baseball bat, he still had the catcher's gear from the summer he had played in a softball league. This had been when he was still married. Liz had told him he needed to make more friends. He pulled down his pants and underwear and placed the crotch protector over his genitals. He put on the chest protector and catcher's mask. He placed the staple gun in his right pants pocket and the knife in the left pocket. He put the pepper spray underneath the chest protector in his shirt pocket.

He picked up one of the extra-large bags of dog food and hauled it to the basement door. He then went into the living room, where he picked up the CD player and a CD of classical music, and then placed those next to the basement door. He went back to the garage and grabbed the snow shovel. He would use the shovel to clean up the chimpanzee shit at the same time that he blasted classical music into the basement to help condition their monkey brains for the crash course in humanization that they were about to receive. Finally, he went to the kitchen and grabbed a bunch of bananas. He hoped that if the chimps associated him with their food supply, they would not want to harm him. He was now ready to make his first descent into his destiny, which was inextricably linked to that of his simian brothers.

He walked carefully and slowly down the steps, carrying the bag of dog food with the bananas on top, against his chest. Again, there was the smell of monkey shit, but it wasn't as bad. It had permeated into his kitchen and living room, so he was getting used to it. When he reached the basement floor, he dropped the bag. He turned to his left to face the chimps, who were huddled in a group in the corner.

He tossed the bananas one by one so that each one landed just in front of the group. The chimps did not move but continued to stare directly at him. Finally, the baby chimp darted forward, grabbed a banana, and then quickly retreated back to the pack. The deposed leader slowly walked forward and picked up a banana and then returned to the group and started eating it. He did not peel it. He ate it whole. Turk had always wondered how chimps ate bananas and whether they peeled off the skin like humans. Now he knew. Eventually, the other chimps did the same, each one moving slowly, lethargically. Turk felt disappointed and slightly depressed. His first encounter as their leader did not even come close to what he had envisioned would be his first triumphal descent into their new reality. But he knew this process would take time.

His first priority was to tend to what went in and what came out: food, water, shit, and piss. Turk walked backward to the glass sliding door, watching the group for any sudden moves. He went outside into the cold, grabbed the hose, twisted the nozzle to turn on the water, and ran back into the basement. He placed the hose into one of the troughs and filled it with water. He emptied the bag of dog food into the other trough. The chimps continued to stare. They remained still. They would eventually become dependent on him as he provided their daily manna.

He went to the top of the stairs to retrieve the snow shovel and the CD player and disc. He placed the CD player on the floor, loaded the disc, cranked up the base, and turned the volume up to high. The intricate sounds and rhythms that had lasted throughout the ages blared from the speakers like rock music. He began shoveling the monkey shit. Once he had gathered the feces into a heap, he had to decide what to do with it. The obvious answer was to shovel it outside onto the patio. But it was cold out there, and Turk did not want to risk leaving the sliding door open for any extended period of time in case one of the chimps was tempted to try to overwhelm him and escape.

The house was heated by a gas furnace with a pilot light at its base. It was walled off from the rest of the basement. There was an open space next to it. Turk opened the door. This would be the perfect place to store the shit temporarily. As he shoveled the shit into the furnace room, his nostrils filled with the smell of feces as the sublime sounds from the ages blasted to a crescendo.

When Turk emerged from the basement, it was dark. He did not know what time it was. As he went through his routine to check that all appliances were turned off and all doors were locked, he realized that he had forgotten to close the garage door. When he went into the garage, he noticed a police car in front of his house, driving slowly down the street. He had never observed cops patrolling in this shell of a neighborhood. The cop did not have the car's headlights on. Turk stood in the middle of the garage and stared out into the darkness. The overhead light exposed him. The vehicle kept creeping forward. He could not see inside the windows but could discern the emergency lights on top. This was definitely a cop car. Turk opened the passenger door to his car, reached inside, and hit the remote to the automatic garage door. It slowly descended as the cop car rolled deeper into the darkness.

32

Turk managed to get only a few hours of sleep that night. He tried to shut down his thoughts but kept ruminating on the next steps of his grand plan. He had woken up at about five thirty to take a piss. He pulled himself out of bed around six because he was unable to fall back asleep. He chugged his first cup of coffee. With the second cup, he popped a diet supplement pill that was an over-the-counter stimulant loaded with caffeine. He had just added this to his morning regimen. Not only did it help curb his appetite, but it also gave him a jolt of energy.

During the course of the night, he had decided that his first step would be to teach the chimps a standardized greeting for their group. He knew from his research that chimps were social. They had grooming rituals. They greeted each other by touching hands, hugging, or kissing. He would start with a simple motion like raising their right paws above their heads like a salute or, better yet, a blessing. He would teach them to bless each other and in so doing, identify themselves as a part of this group of special chimps. This would serve a useful purpose in and of itself and also serve as the foundation upon which he could teach higher-level activities.

He picked up a bunch of bananas. He would use the bananas to reinforce the actions he would be training the chimps to emulate. He put on his protective gear, gathered his weapons, and once again descended into the basement, where he once again found the chimps nestled in the corner. He felt less fear this time. He walked over to the group. He pried off one banana from the bunch and put the rest on the floor. The chimps all looked up at him. He raised his right hand over his head with his arm outstretched. This was a preview. There was no reaction to his standing there so close, invading their space, and thankfully, no sudden moves to try to take him out.

As he looked down at the chimps, he realized he had no plan as to how to get them to raise their right paws. If he couldn't get them to do that, then there was no way he could reinforce the action by giving them a banana. He noticed the baby chimp sitting at the front of the group. He looked up at Turk with wide round eyes. Maybe he would be receptive. Turk could teach him the motion in front of the other chimps. That would be a start.

He kneeled down facing the baby chimp and, using his left hand, raised the chimp's right arm over his head. With his right hand, Turk grabbed a banana and placed it within a few inches of the chimp's face. The chimp took a bite. Turk repeated the action two more times.

Turk grabbed another banana. This time, he waited until he had released the arm and, while it still lingered overhead, he stuck the banana in the chimp's face, and the chimp kept his arm extended overhead as he devoured the fruit. Turk did this two more times, and each time the chimp held his paw up a little longer. Turk felt satisfied. He went back upstairs. He had accomplished something in his first lesson. This was a solid base upon which he could build.

33

It was Monday morning, and Turk was back in his cubicle. He hadn't slept much the night before, like so many other nights since he had lost his wife and children. Before leaving the house, he had taken his diet supplement along with a cup of black coffee. He had stopped at a gas station on the way into work and bought a large cup of coffee and two cream donuts, which he had consumed in the car.

The implementation of the PPP wasn't starting out as he had envisioned. He was more like a janitor than a leader. Cleaning up chimpanzee shit and piss was necessary, especially in the beginning, so that was to be expected. But what he had not anticipated was the fear that he was experiencing as he tried to domesticate these wild beasts, who as it turned out were more animal than human. He had previously thought of them as more human than animal. But they were big and strong and quick and had sharp claws and teeth and no empathy for Turk or any other humans. They had no clue about what Turk was trying to do for them, how he was trying to elevate them.

Still, Turk was not a quitter. He had listened to plenty of CDs on goal setting. One had to plan right from the beginning that unexpected obstacles would arise and need to be overcome. And it was how he, Turk, William Malone, dealt with these setbacks that would ultimately define his legacy.

After having been out of the office for two days, he had some emails to catch up on, but nothing had changed. It was the same boring routine, only this morning it was easier to take because he knew his time in this hellhole would be ending in the not too distant future as he developed the chimps in his own image. The dream was becoming a reality. He cruised through the day on autopilot and a sugar and caffeine-induced high, nothing new, nothing challenging, just more of the same, like the hands of a watch that continually rotated past the same twelve hours twice a day, day after day. The other constant was the annoying scent of Evelyn's candles.

This coming weekend was Turk's turn to have the kids stay with him if he and Liz were splitting parenting time according to the settlement agreement they had signed but to which Liz had not adhered. Although he desperately wanted to see them, he wasn't sure if it was feasible with a basement full of chimpanzees. And if he sent Liz a text stating he intended to pick them up this weekend, it was almost a certainty that she would come up with yet another excuse as to why the kids could not come visit. He decided it would work out best if he didn't contact her and by default skipped this weekend to allow time for the transition and for things to calm down.

As he drove home from work, he checked his rearview mirror. There was a police car immediately behind him. His entire body locked up. He could barely control the steering wheel. The cop continued to follow him as he drove past a stretch of huge hardware stores, gigantic retail outlets, and megagrocery stores. Everything was supersized. In front of him, everything was limitless. Behind him lurked potential disaster. Turk shifted his attention repeatedly between the road ahead and the cop behind him. He thought he could feel his heart palpitating. Then suddenly, the cop turned into a fast-food restaurant. And he was gone, at least for now.

That evening, Turk suited up in his catcher's gear and went down into the basement. The baby chimp was sitting on the rug underneath the poster of Hanuman. The rest of the pack was huddled together in what had become their usual place in the corner. When the baby chimp saw Turk, he came running over to him with his right paw raised high above his head. Turk couldn't believe it! The chimp obviously wanted a banana. Turk ran upstairs and returned with the chimp's Cub Scout shirt and more bananas.

He worked the chimp's paws through the shirt sleeves and buttoned it. The chimp raised its right arm and kept it high in the air, and Turk gave him another banana. After finishing its second banana, the chimp raised his arm a third time, and Turk gave him yet another banana.

Turk lifted the baby chimp up and placed him about halfway up the stairs so the other chimps could see him. It was the baby chimp who was setting the example for them to follow. As Turk looked up at the chimp in the uniform with his paw raised high, it struck him that it appeared as if the chimp was possibly giving a blessing to his brother chimpanzees or doing a Nazi salute.

Before going back upstairs, Turk refilled the troughs of dog food and water. He then shoveled the monkey shit that had accumulated over the last couple of days and deposited it on the heap of shit in the space next to the furnace.

The next evening after work, he suited up and went back down into the basement with a bunch of bananas. Yet again, the chimps were sitting in a group in the corner of the basement. They had obviously gotten up and moved since he last saw them, because he could see feces scattered all across the floor. As he had done the night before, the baby chimp came over to him and raised his arm. Turk immediately gave him a banana. In that moment, it occurred to him that although he thought he was training the chimp, perhaps the baby chimp thought that he was controlling Turk's behavior. That was a consequence he had never intended or anticipated. But more important, how was he going to motivate the adult chimps?

He decided he would start by trying to train the chimps to shit in the trough of cat litter rather than all over the basement floor. He went over to the trough and started to pantomime how to take a dump. He bent over and stuck his butt out over the tub of cat litter. He grunted and tensed his body like he was straining to expel a turd. He then grabbed a banana, pulled off his catcher's mask, put the banana to his mouth, and chomped his jaws up and down as he ate it. He put his mask back on and approached the group, holding out the banana in front of them. They sat motionless and looked at him with blank stares. He was trying to show them that if they shit or pissed in the trough, they would get a reward, but it was not registering in their chimp brains. He went through the routine a second time but still got no reaction.

The baby chimp approached him again, turned his back to the tub, and bent over, mimicking Turk's actions. He stood up and extended his arm above his head, clearly expecting to get another banana, which Turk gave him instantly. Turk went back to the group and held up the bunch of bananas, hoping to entice one of them to follow the lead of the baby chimp, but yet again, he got no response.

He went back upstairs and into the garage to get the snow shovel. He closed the basement door behind him. When he returned, the baby chimp was standing in the hallway. He had seen Turk open the door and was able to mimic that movement and open the door himself.

Turk went back downstairs, and the baby chimp followed. Turk took the snow shovel, scooped up the shit on the floor, and once again deposited it onto the heap next to the furnace.

The following evening after work, on the way to his house, Turk stopped again at Big Ray's. He bought a doggie bed and a cat litter box. He decided he was going to move the baby chimp out of the basement and into the command center in his office that opened to the living room. He also bought a baby high chair. Turk had a piano in his living room. He had already purchased the *Beginning Piano* book. He decided his next step with the baby chimp was to teach him how to play. He needed the high chair so the chimp would be able to sit up high enough to reach the keys.

34

Over the next two weeks, Turk put in his time at the office during the day and worked with the baby chimp at night. The transition to his office went smoothly. There was no need to wear his protective gear when interacting with only the baby chimp. Turk had enticed the baby chimp out of the basement with bananas. The chimp had adapted readily to his own comfortable bed, and Turk had made progress training him to shit in the litter box. When Turk awoke that morning, he found, for the first time, a chimp turd in the box.

He also began teaching the chimp how to play the piano. Turk started by propping the chimp up to the piano in the high chair and placing a bunch of bananas on top of the piano. He stroked the key in the exact middle of the keyboard. He took the chimp's paw, pried his index finger upward, and pushed the same key with the chimp's finger. Then he gave the chimp a banana.

Turk repeated this action countless times, gradually reducing the incentive from a whole banana to a bite of banana, until the chimp began to stroke the keyboard on his own, followed by a bite of banana. Turk then went from one keystroke to a second keystroke on the next highest key using the chimp's middle finger, to a third keystroke on the next highest key using the chimp's third finger, and kept adding more strokes. They had worked up seven keystrokes to the note B. The baby chimp had almost learned the entire C scale.

During this period, Turk had also suited up and descended into the basement every evening. There was no progress. The group of adult chimps didn't separate from their huddle in the corner and did not show any reaction to Turk's presence. He dutifully refilled their troughs of food and water and shoveled their shit into the heap next to the furnace.

It had been months since he'd had any contact with his kids. He felt that he had his situation with the chimps under sufficient control that he could handle having them for the weekend. And he knew they would love seeing the baby chimp. Turk sent Liz a text asking if he could pick up the kids on Saturday morning.

On the way home from work that that evening, like every other evening, he drove past the Wiley Rascal's Pub. This time, he decided he would stop and go in. He had made great progress with the baby chimp. He believed he would be able to figure out how to break through to the adult chimps. He deserved a break and a reward for all that he had accomplished. And once he had completed the PPP, he would fit right in here.

Even though it was a weeknight, the parking lot was full. Inside, the place was packed. He maneuvered through the crowd and found the only open seat at the bar. He looked around and could see people sitting together at tables, laughing, drinking beer and imported wine, and eating expensive food. A sense of gaiety permeated the atmosphere. He could see patrons slapping each other on their backs. No doubt, in a collective, alcohol-induced euphoria, one of them had made a witty, insightful remark. And after everyone stopped laughing, someone else chimed in with the perfect retort. Timing was everything, after all.

Turk had not realized that right around the corner from his office, the site of so much drudgery, existed one of those ubiquitous places where happiness and pleasure were being manufactured and could be purchased like any other commodity. The owners of the pub had found a need, or maybe a desire, or both, and were making a lot of money filling that need.

It was like everyone in the place was one of the popular kids in high school. Turk recalled that there had been that one group of kids who always hung out together, and everyone else had wanted to be a part of that group. There had actually been two groups, one male and one female, that were mirror images of each other. Each group had always sat in the same place at lunch in the cafeteria. The tables were set up in rows. Each row consisted of three tables with attached benches for seating that could be folded up for storage. Once unfolded, the tables fell into place end to end to create one long table that could seat comfortably as many as six students per table with space for eighteen lunch trays.

The popular group had always sat at the center table. Those of lesser social status had crammed into the adjoining tables and tried to get as close as they could to the center. No one had ever sat in the spaces reserved for the popular kids, except the popular kids. They had staked out their territory and their place at the top of the hierarchy.

Nobody on the outside had really known what they did or where they went on the weekends. The kids who were allowed to hang out on the fringes may have had some idea, but to the rest, like Turk, it had been almost mythical. On Mondays, each special group had huddled together, privately. No outsiders were allowed in, only the elite. They had probably talked about where they had gone and what fun things they had done together. They had probably gathered at the home of one of the popular kids, whichever kid had parents who were gone for the night or the weekend, and had wild parties. They had probably known older kids who could buy them liquor. They had probably driven around and hooked up with the cool kids from other high schools who were handsome and beautiful just like they were. The possibilities of a sexual encounter, of excitement, of adventure, had always been around the corner. So when Turk walked into this bar, he was stepping into all that. And it wouldn't be long until he would fit right in and could take his rightful place among the elite.

The waiters and waitresses hurried past, balancing full trays of drinks over their heads. Television sets were mounted everywhere. Turk could not hear them. The sound was muted. One would normally expect to see sports channels playing, but tonight it was all news. Turk could see reporters standing in a remote location, apparently broadcasting reports of impending war or a terrorist act in some distant place. The images on the TVs were simply part of the background, and no one was watching.

The man sitting at the bar next to him started talking. He had a slight paunch around his belly and gray hair on his temples. Turk could barely hear him over the din of the crowd and the loud music playing in the background. It wasn't an actual conversation. The guy didn't really talk to Turk; he didn't listen or interact. He just quacked away like a duck. His mouth flipped open and closed, and sound came out. The content was irrelevant. Turk did learn that the guy was a failed dentist. Turk was surprised. He had never met one before. He didn't know it ever happened to dentists.

He had always thought that once people graduated with degrees in medicine or dentistry or law, after all that hard work, they were set for life. And he always felt inadequate because he didn't have a graduate degree. As a claims adjuster, he dealt with lawyers almost every day, and they always acted like they were superior to him. But he never realized that getting an advanced degree was only the beginning, that there were so many people out there with graduate degrees, and that just getting the degree was no guarantee of success.

And he knew firsthand, dealing with attorneys, that a law degree did not necessarily equate to a high degree of intelligence. As a claims adjuster, he had heard the old cliché numerous times: What do you call the person who graduated last in their class from medical school? A doctor. So what was this dentist doing here? He had nothing on Turk. Was he clinging desperately to a lost sense of self-esteem? Was he a fraud? And what about all the others in the bar who appeared so happy and jolly? And, Turk had to ask himself, why was he here?

35

That evening, he suited up and descended once again into the basement. And once again, the chimps were huddled in the corner. He had his toolbox and a stepladder. He picked up the video camera off the floor and examined it. It appeared to be intact. He placed the stepladder underneath the mount for the camera hanging from the ceiling and positioned it so that he was facing the chimps. He climbed to the top so he was standing about three feet in the air. He reached up to the ceiling and reinstalled the camera. As he stood above the chimps, extended, he felt vulnerable. He worked quickly. When he finished, he grabbed the ladder and his toolbox and backed up slowly toward the stairs. He walked backward up the stairs, careful not to turn his back on the chimps.

Turk went to his desk and logged onto his computer. The baby chimp was sitting in his doggie bed. Turk clicked on the video camera icon, and a view of the basement flashed on the screen. The chimps were not huddled in the corner but were milling around. He could see that the deposed leader had ascended to the top of the stairs and appeared to be tugging at the door. Using his computer keys, Turk was able to adjust the angle of the camera and zoom in for a closer look. The chimp was jostling the door and trying to turn the doorknob. Thank God he had installed the deadbolt.

The chimp appeared to have noticed the movement of the camera. In an instant, he lunged at it. His paws were extended. His face filled the entire computer screen with a menacing glare. In that moment, Turk could see the chimp's sharp teeth and glimpse deep into his dark, empty eyes. The screen went blank. Turk could hear the sound of the camera as it crashed onto the basement floor.

When he arrived at the office the next morning, he noticed a police car parked in the adjacent lot in front of a title company. He had never spotted a police car there in the past. Could this be a setup? He went to the restroom before going to his cube. There was another coworker at the urinal next to him. This meant that after Turk washed his hands and used the moist paper towel to grasp the door handle, he would not be able to prop the door open with his foot and throw the wet wad into the trash bin. Instead, he would have to shove it into his pocket and discard it in the wastebasket at his desk. He walked past the receptionist on his way to his cube. She did not look up or acknowledge his presence.

Smitty had scheduled a staff meeting at eight thirty. This was the first one since his arrival. Turk arrived early at quarter after eight. When he logged onto his computer, there was a meeting invite from Smitty for nine thirty the next morning in his office. Turk froze. Was Smitty on to him? What did he know? Had he figured it all out, the little prick? Turk had been so careful not to leave any tracks. Was this guy really that good? Possibly. Smitty was thorough. He was a thorough prick.

He might already have gathered the evidence that would prove Turk guilty beyond a reasonable doubt of committing insurance fraud. Smitty had probably contacted corporate and invoked their vast powers. They had probably already done an audit and were in possession of copies of the entire document trail. Had Jenny from the bank tipped them off? Was she part of this?

Turk realized that when he walked into Smitty's office the next day, it could be the moment when life as he knew it would end. This was when it could all finally catch up with him, the regrets and resentments that had piled up, the fatal flaws in his personality, and the ultimate mistake—crossing the line into criminal activity.

He accepted the invitation. He had no choice. He would walk calmly into Smitty's office to face his fate with dignity and grace. The next message was an email from Smitty. Turk braced himself and clicked on the message. It was a group email to all the claims adjusters in the office.

> It has been six months now since I took over the management of this office. I have sent invites to all you scheduling meetings to go over the performance appraisals that I have prepared for each of you. These will take place tomorrow. Please be prompt.

Turk felt like someone had taken hundreds of nano drill bits, implanted them into the top of his skull, swirled them at a high rate of speed, and flushed out his nervous system from his brain down through his toes. So they had not discovered his crime. He had not been singled out.

A wonderful tingling sensation pulsated throughout his entire body, an exquisite feeling of electricity flowing through every nerve. For an instant, the protective sheath that encased his ego and sense of self-identity became permeable, and he thought he could feel a spirit descend and envelope his entire being. He felt whole, intact, and connected to something beyond himself. He didn't know what it was. He thought he could speak in any language, even ones he previously had not known existed. Then the feeling vanished. He tried to hold on to it, but it was gone.

As Turk and his coworkers filed into the conference room, he turned to one of his fellow adjusters and raised his eyebrows.

"This should be interesting," he said sarcastically.

The guy looked at him but did not respond.

Everyone was seated and at attention at 8:28 a.m., looking at an empty podium. Smitty did not arrive until ten minutes later. When he made his entrance, he strutted to the lectern and turned to face his audience. It appeared to Turk that Smitty was expecting everyone to applaud or at least make some type of acknowledgment, but they all sat silent and motionless, staring straight ahead. Smitty wasn't getting any better of a reaction than Turk experienced every evening with his chimps.

"It's nice to see everyone here this morning," said Smitty. "As you know, I have scheduled meetings with each of you to go over your six-month evaluations, that is, six months since I took over. I thought it would be helpful for you to have this meeting so that you can get a chance to know me a little better, how I think and what my expectations are for you."

There was no reaction.

"Let me start by issuing a challenge to each of you, individually and as part of the American Security team. You will recall that when I first got here, I met with each of you and asked this question: What is it that *you* can do to be the best claims representative that *you* can be? I'm sure you have all given it a lot of thought. So let me ask you this: As you begin to build a better *you*, what is the foundation upon which you will rebuild the new *you* to be the best darn claims representative in this company? That's what we are all striving for, isn't that right?"

Again there was no response.

Just like in his first meeting with Smitty, Turk found himself fighting off an overwhelming visceral urge to get up and slap the little shithead. In addition to that, this was not even original material. Turk had read it or heard it before. It was buried somewhere in his vast collection of self-help resources. He couldn't recall the specific title, but he felt intuitively, instinctively, that he knew the answer. So he would play along.

"I think I know the answer," said Turk. He realized he was talking too loudly.

"You know the answer?" responded Smitty.

"Yes. I know the answer."

"So what is the answer?"

"The answer is … attitude."

"Yes. Attitude is the answer," Smitty said. "First, you have to have the right attitude. You have to think right. If you think right, then you will act right and you will do right."

Turk knew where Smitty was going. This was not a new philosophy that Smitty had developed. It was just the same recycled bullshit that Turk had heard from his claims managers in the past. The whole point of being a claims adjuster was to be a tight-ass. If you moved up in the hierarchy, it was simply a matter of perfecting that art and finding new and different ways to contract the sphincter a little tighter.

"We've done statistical studies," continued Smitty. "We've looked at jury verdicts all over the country. We've analyzed them and reduced them to a mathematical formula. And it's clear. Historically, we have been overpaying claims, all claims—the big ones, the little ones, claims with merit, and frivolous claims.

"We are giving these claimants and their greedy attorneys a free ride. And at whose expense? All of us. Who pays the price? We pay the price. You and me. Think of it like a huge cesspool. Every time we overpay a claim to one single individual, the premiums for all of us go up. We all pay more. And the cesspool rises."

Smitty was getting worked up. He started talking louder and gesturing with his hands.

"We all pay more, so we save less. We invest less in our futures. That shrinks the national economy, so there are fewer jobs. There is more poverty. So more people need public assistance. So our taxes go up. So we pay it out the ass yet a second time, first in premiums, next in taxes. It's a vicious cycle. This, of course, is demoralizing and, in turn, contributes to the moral decay and sense of hopelessness that we see overtaking our society today ..."

Smitty spoke so forcefully that it appeared he actually believed what he was saying. Or was this just an act? Turk knew Smitty was only out for himself. His only concern was making his numbers look good so he could get the next promotion. A small pocket of saliva started to form in the corner of his mouth.

"Let me ask you this: If you go into a court of law, which is where these claims all end up if they don't get settled, who bears the burden of proof?"

Turk was not sure if this was a rhetorical question or if Smitty expected someone to respond. So Turk continued to play along.

"I think I know the answer."

Smitty seemed distracted. "You know the answer?"

"Yes. I know the answer."

"So what is the answer?"

"The answer is ... the burden of proof is on the claimant."

"Yes. That's exactly right! It is the plaintiff, at every turn, not the defendant, who bears the burden of proof. Indeed, we could go to court and not utter even one word in defense of our insured, and we could still win if the plaintiff has not proven his or her case. And I'm not saying that's a good strategy, but are you with me on this?"

Again, everyone besides Turk sat silent and motionless.

"I'm with you!" said Turk. He realized he may have responded a bit too loudly.

Smitty paused.

"Well ... good, Mr. Malone. Thank you. So the new philosophy is we never give them the benefit of any doubt. We, the claims representatives, are empowered to be the new *minijurors*. If these claimants deserve any money, let them prove up every last dime. Let them prove it to us. Make them meet their burden of proof!"

While everyone else continued to sit motionless, Turk bobbed his head up and down.

"Upper management in the home office has studied this. They have this worked out to a precise mathematical equation. And like any formula, there are variables. They have taken into account all the various factors: type of claimant, severity of the injury, whether the claimant has hired an attorney, the population, whether rural or a big city, the state where the injury occurred. All these and other factors were figured in. And do you know what the biggest factor was?"

He paused and looked around the room.

"The biggest factor was … you! Our studies bear out that the claims representatives with the highest performance appraisals, that is 'exceeds expectations,' obtained the cheapest settlements compared to their counterparts who received a 'meets expectations' or 'did not meet expectations.' The most important variable in this equation is *you* and your fellow professional claims representatives. Have I made myself clear on this point?"

"Yes! Absolutely crystal clear!" said Turk. He realized that he was almost shouting. He lowered his voice. "I can assure you that I will invariably do my part."

Smitty paused again. "Thank you, Mr. Malone. I'm sure that you speak for the entire office. In closing, I wanted to answer a question that a lot of you may be asking yourselves: What is Mr. Smith doing to be the best claims manager, the best leader, the best Allen S. Smith, that he can be?"

Turk had never asked himself that question.

"I want you to know that I have reflected on this a lot over the last few days. And I have concluded that *Allen* can be the best *Allen* that *Allen* can be by helping each of you to be the best darn claims representative that you can be. And how can Allen do this? Allen can lead by example. Allen can listen to find out what your needs are and what he can do to help you meet the company's expectations. Leading is listening, leading is learning, leading is serving."

This all sounded familiar to Turk. He remembered where Smitty had gotten his entire spiel. He had listened to one of the classics: *Once, Twice, Three Times a Leader: The Pyramid Paradigm for Effective Management.* It was not only a guide for motivating deadbeat employees, but it also explained the persuasive power of phrasing key points in threes.

Turk was glad he would only have to deal with this bullshit for a little longer. All he had to do now was play it safe and hang on. Soon, he would be out of there. And just in time. It was getting harder to hide in that C– to C+ range that had been his territory for so long. Smitty and his gang did not just want his eight hours a day. They wanted his soul.

36

That evening, Turk suited up and descended once again into the basement. And once again, the chimps were huddled in the corner. He still had not figured out a way to break through to them. He was no longer sure that he wanted to continue to make the effort. Were they secretly plotting a rebellion? Did he need to watch out for an escape attempt or some kind or a trap? He shoveled the monkey shit and deposited it in the heap next to the furnace. He refilled the troughs of dog food and water.

After he had finished in the basement, he gave another piano lesson to the baby chimp. Turk created a name for him, Bellzak, a word that would someday be known as a Turkism. It meant "maker of beautiful background music." Turk worked with Bellzak on stroking the next key, which was the high C. When Bellzak completed the task, Turk gave him a bite of banana. The baby chimp could now play the scale from low C to high C.

Turk grabbed the chimp's right index finger, went back to the low C, grabbed his second and third fingers and stroked three keys in a row: C, then up to D, and then up to E, using a different finger for each key. He gave the chimp another bite of banana. Turk repeated that process two more times. Turk then placed Bellzak's index finger just above the low C key and released his hands from the chimp's paws. On his own, Bellzak stroked all three keys in succession using his first, second, and third fingers.

"Bellzak, you are awesome!" shouted Turk. He gave him an entire banana.

Later that night, Turk settled into the recliner in his office. He had given up trying to fall sleep in his bed upstairs. Like so many other nights, he could not shut down his thoughts. He was dreading his meeting with Smitty the next morning. He still had not heard back from Liz about picking up the kids this weekend.

As he got ready for work the next morning, he chugged a cup of espresso and popped a diet supplement pill. On the way to work, he stopped at the No Turn on Red sign, not wanting to take the chance of a cop pulling him over with a basement full of chimpanzees at home. Then, at a gas station, he bought three cream-filled donuts and a large cup of coffee. When he arrived at the office, the sugar, caffeine, and adrenaline were all pumping through his veins in unison. He was ready for his meeting with Smitty.

When Turk arrived at Smitty's office, he was on the phone. He motioned for Turk to come in. He took a break from the call, handed Turk the appraisal, and told him to read it. He went back to the conversation and talked for another five to ten minutes.

The appraisal was a complete work of fiction. It was obvious to him that Smitty had no idea what he had been doing. Anyone's name could have been at the top of the first page. The categories ranged from job knowledge to customer service to teamwork. There were three choices for each category: does not meet expectations, meets expectations, or exceeds expectations. Smitty had checked the box for meets expectations in each category. In the comments section at the end, Smitty wrote: *Bill needs to keep striving to be the best Bill that Bill can be.*

After Smitty finished the call, he turned to Turk. "Any questions?"

After the speech the day before, Turk was expecting more, perhaps some sage advice or some mentoring, maybe some leading by serving speech.

"Not really," said Turk. "But I'm a little curious about how you came up with these ratings. Did you review any of the files that I worked on?"

"Well, I didn't do a formal audit of anyone's files. I looked at a number of things and based the appraisal on my general observations."

"Okay. I'm sure you realize the importance of these appraisals to all the claims representatives, myself included."

"Absolutely."

"I mean, our raises are based on this. Our standing with American Security is based on this. Our futures, basically, for each of us, and again, myself included, everything is based on what your opinion is of who we are and our value to this company."

"Yes. I realize that, and I take that responsibility seriously."

"So I guess I was wondering, is there nothing that I exceed in? I mean, I always comply with the prompt contact policy and always file my reports by the deadlines."

"Well, Bill, I'm sure you don't understand this from corporate's viewpoint, from the management perspective …"

Once again, Turk felt the urge to lunge across the desk and slap that patronizing goofy little motherfucker.

"Following the prompt contact policy, submitting reports timely—these are the types of things we expect. So when you comply with the company's policies and procedures, you are simply meeting expectations.

"Now, if I were to give you an exceeds in any category, I would have to justify it with a lengthy supporting memo citing examples and the reasons behind my recommendation. And that entails a lot of effort. So that's on you and the other claims reps. If you go above and beyond, it should be obvious. And you should send me an email advising me of your accomplishments. With that information, the supporting memo would be a quick and easy one for me to write."

"But you never told us that was the company's procedure," said Turk.

"Well, that should be obvious," said Smitty.

"So did anyone get an exceeds on anything?" asked Turk.

"Well, Bill, you know I can't talk about the ratings I have given to the other reps. But let me just say that, in general, the group of claims reps in this office, including you, are average. And you need to understand, in my eyes and the eyes of corporate, that is a good thing. You all meet expectations. You all fit the mold. And we don't have any bad actors or troublemakers here.

"And, Bill, to your credit, you are as bland and unremarkable as the other reps. Indistinguishable, really. You are all interchangeable, like replacement parts for a car. If you or one of the other reps goes down, you know, retires, quits, gets fired, or whatever, maybe goes on medical leave, there is another one there to take your place. And that is how we want it. We don't need any prima donnas around here. That just breeds discontent.

"We are not grooming you to be exceptional. That's not what we need. We need workers who can do the tasks required by the jobs and be content with their jobs and their salaries. And, Bill, I am pleased to inform you that you fit right in. I would have to say that you are not just average, you are very average. In fact, if I had to give you a rating for this criterion, I would say that you are exceedingly average."

37

Turk knew instantly that it was him. He had read about it but had never thought he would experience it. He was standing in the produce section of Big Ray's, where he had come to buy another crate of bananas. He had barely slept the previous night. He was pumped up on the caffeine and sugar that carried him through the day and had become his routine. But it didn't matter. This was real. This was valid. This was bona fide.

That punk Smitty didn't know jack shit. Turk was not average. He gave the appearance of being normal, but he was not mediocre. And this was proof. Turk was one of the chosen few. This was a Felix sighting. Turk's idol had not died. As many of his fans believed he had just disappeared in an attempt to escape the overwhelming fame and notoriety that had created so much chaos in his life and driven him to drugs and close to the edge of insanity.

This was not the image of Felix in his prime, the one etched forever into the collective consciousness. This guy was older. He had a few wrinkles on his face. His hair was gray and cut short. It no longer hung down around his shoulders. But this was definitely Felix. He was still alive. And Turk was a witness.

Felix disappeared around the next aisle. Turk followed him to the frozen food section but kept his distance. The figure opened the door to the freezer, and Turk could see his breath. The door frosted over, blurring Turk's view. Felix stepped forward closer to the freezer and reached inside. As the icy, frigid air blew back over him, he glowed as if he were radioactive. The brilliance was too intense for Turk's eyes. He squinted and then ducked back behind the shelf filled with boxes of macaroni and cheese.

Turk looked back around the corner, but Felix was gone. Turk tried to process what he had just seen. This guy had looked like an older version of Felix. Therefore, Felix must not have died. Or maybe this was just some guy who looked like an older version of Felix and Turk had embellished what he had seen to the point that he believed he had seen Felix. Turk knew he had pumped huge amounts of sugar and caffeine into his body and that he had not slept well in a long time, but he still felt like he had a grip on reality. But was it starting to slip away? Was he losing his mind? That was a scary possibility. He thought he knew the difference between the real world he lived in and the dreams that could be intruding into his waking life.

He decided he had to try to talk to Felix. How could he pass up this opportunity to meet his idol? He started searching through the aisles in the store. When he didn't see Felix, he started frantically combing through the rows of groceries at a faster pace. Felix wasn't there. He abandoned his cart and ran out into the parking lot. There was still no Felix. He had disappeared.

38

Another two weeks passed as Turk sleepwalked through his daily routine at the office. Every evening, Turk obsessively peeked through the blinds in his home office at least three times to see if he could spot the cop spying on him. So far, he had not seen the cop car, but that didn't mean the cop was not still staking him out. Was this something he really needed to fear, or was he just being paranoid? These disturbing thoughts were similar to the thoughts that had spontaneously burst into his consciousness when he was an adolescent.

He spent every evening shoveling shit and working with Bellzak on the piano. This night would be special, though. They had mastered the C scale from low to high and had started working back down from high to low, using all five fingers on Bellzak's right paw. Bellzak was only three keys away from being able to play the entire C scale. Turk took the baby chimp's right little finger and placed it on the high C. On his own, Bellzak hit every key using all his fingers as he descended down the scale to the low C. Turk gave him a banana.

The next step would be crucial, not only for Bellzak but for the realization of Turk's dream. Forget the adult chimps languishing in the basement; they were a bunch of lowlife primates with no ambition. Turk needed just one chimp, the baby chimp. Turk decided to demonstrate to Bellzak what he wanted him to do. Turk placed his right thumb on the low C, hit each note using all his fingers as he moved up the scale to the high C, and then went back down to the low C. He took Bellzak's right thumb, placed it on the low C, and then let go. Bellzak played up and down the scale just as Turk had done. Bellzak had played the entire C scale by himself, unassisted!

For this accomplishment, Turk had a surprise. From his shirt pocket he pulled out not a banana, but a giant candy bar. He unwrapped it and held it over Bellzak's head. Bellzak stood up on the high chair, opened his mouth, and reached for it. Turk let it drop. The baby chimp caught it with his teeth and then jumped off the high chair. He scurried several feet away and devoured it in a couple of bites. This was the first time Bellzak had ever eaten processed sugar. He went back to Turk and put his front paws on Turk's lap. He looked up at Turk as if he were asking for more. Turk had a second candy bar, which he unwrapped and tossed into the air. Bellzak chased it down and ate it in an instant.

Turk suited up and descended once again into the basement. He shoveled the monkey shit and deposited it in the heap next to the furnace, but he noticed something different this time. There were scattered patches of chimp fur, which he scooped up along with the turds. He refilled the troughs of dog food and water. Although he had not noticed any decrease in the amount of shit he'd had to shovel, it appeared that the chimps had consumed less that day than usual.

He had not heard back from Liz about a visit by the kids. He had been preoccupied with the PPP. And he knew he couldn't bring them to his house, yet anyway, with a basement full of chimpanzees, but she didn't know any of that. It had been a very long time since he had seen Nick and Alicia, but Liz was the one who had thrown the timing off with her last-minute plans over Thanksgiving and Christmas break. So he thought he would just pick up the kids for the day. He would think of someplace to go. They would eat pizza and ice cream. He should have thought of this sooner. He whipped out his cell phone and typed a message.

> Liz, I have to say that I am disappointed that you never got back to me when I last texted you about picking up the kids. I will be at your house this Saturday morning at 10:00 a.m. to pick them up. Please have them ready to go.

He wouldn't tell her that he only planned to keep the kids for the day until he picked them up. She didn't need to know that right now. He had never missed or even been late on a child support payment. Regardless, he had every right to be with his kinds during his scheduled times.

The next morning, Turk took his company car to the dealership for an oil change and routine maintenance. American Security required everyone with a company car to have this done every three months. He got a ride to work in the courtesy van provided by the dealer, but the dealer only provided that service in the morning. He would have to find other transportation when he went back to pick up his car that evening.

At the end of the workday, his only option was to take the bus. Turk didn't know anyone in the office well enough to ask for a favor, and he didn't want to pay for a taxi. His office was located just off the interstate on the west side of the city. The dealership was on the far north side. What would have been a quick and simple trip if he'd had his car would now be a complex and time-consuming task. First, he had to find out where the nearest bus stop was and when the bus would arrive. Then he would have to navigate the maze of routes and connections.

The bus routes he had to take went through the center of the city and the pockets of poverty there and then out to the suburbs. The ride from his office into downtown was uneventful. He only had to change buses once before arriving at the main terminal. He boarded the next bus. It would take him to within a half mile of the dealership. He found an empty seat near the middle of the bus.

A huge, grossly obese woman sat down in the seat in front of him. She had a child with her, probably around three to four years old. Her hair was greasy, almost matted to her head. Turk could smell the odor of hair spray and deodorant mixed with body odor. The child was barefoot. His belly appeared slightly distended; he was wearing a dirty T-shirt with a tear above his left shoulder. Every thirty seconds or so, he would pound his open palm against the window of the bus and let out a loud, guttural yelp that penetrated to the core of Turk's eardrums. It wasn't human; it was an animal noise. Everyone on the bus looked at the kid. The mother did not react but sat motionless with her back to Turk, facing straight ahead. The kid would not shut up. What was wrong with him?

Finally, the bus arrived at a stop, and the kid and his mother stood up to exit. She grabbed his shirt right where the tear was over his shoulder and lifted him next to her in the aisle. He flailed his arms about wildly and screeched. This was a high-pitched sound that was primitive and several octaves higher than any sound Turk had ever heard.

When Turk was young, he had thought he would have accomplished more by this point in his life. This was not the way it was supposed to have gone. But this poor kid, would he ever be able to achieve even the level of existence that Turk found so frustrating? He was only three or four years old. Had the die already been cast? Had the mold already hardened?

The stop closest to the dealership was about five blocks away at the intersection of two four-lane roads. Both streets were lined with businesses, each surrounded by its own parking lot. Turk's first task was to cross eight lanes of traffic moving at thirty-five or forty miles an hour. No one seemed to notice him standing, stranded, on the curb. He had to wait for the light to turn red. As he stepped into the street, a car accelerated and then turned in front of him within only a couple of feet. It was making a left turn on the green arrow. Turk had done it countless times in his car. But now he had no vehicle surrounding him, no metal shield, nothing to put him on equal footing with everyone else. He darted to the other side of the intersection.

Then he had to hike along the edge of another busy street. He passed an insurance agency and several houses that had been converted into small businesses, each one surrounded by a small patch of grass and each with a huge sign in front. The gravel strip on which he was walking next to the road narrowed so that the oncoming traffic to his left whipped past him within just a foot or two. A rock slipped into his shoe, and he felt a twinge of pain with each step, forcing him to shift more of his weight forward to the ball of his foot and throwing him off balance as the cars continually sped past.

When he finally reached the dealership, he still had to walk another block across the parking lot to get to the service department. The asphalt was decaying, and he had to walk around numerous craters of varying sizes filled with gravel and chunks of blacktop, but the ordeal of getting his car repaired was almost over. In the distance, he could see Big Ray's face mounted high on top of another one of his superstores.

Alone on the bus, among the faceless masses, in the most destitute and dangerous part of the city, and without his car, he had felt isolated and vulnerable, even more so when he had to walk the half mile to the dealership, a pedestrian walking in the dark along the side of the road in a deteriorating suburban landscape with no sidewalks.

When researching the PPP, he had read an article about alpha gorillas in the wild. If a young, ambitious, aggressive gorilla challenged the leader and lost, he would be banished from the community and forced to live alone in the forest. He could empathize with his huge wild primate cousins. He was out there. He was alone. And he was exposed. He could not seek any protection from the pack or the herd. And he had a basement full of wild animals who were not content and could be on the verge of busting out at any moment.

39

Turk had not been down into the basement for probably three days. He suited up and descended into the basement to shovel more shit. The chimps were grouped together in the corner, as they always were. But this time, they were all lying on the floor. None of them were standing or even sitting. He couldn't tell if they were awake. They looked emaciated, and there was chimp fur scattered around the basement. The food and water troughs were full, and there was no shit on the floor.

What he had suspected was possible all along was now obvious: the Nigerians had sold him a pack of diseased chimpanzees. That was probably why Turk had been able to defeat the chimp's leader in hand-to-paw combat. He thought he could outscam the scammers, but he had been suckered.

As he walked through the basement, he could feel the soles of his shoes stick to the grime that had accumulated from the remnants of shit and piss that had been excreted onto the basement floor. He opened the glass sliding door to the patio and grabbed the hose. He squeezed the nozzle and sprayed down the entire cement floor in the direction of the drain that was next to the furnace. The drain was clogged, and the water backed up into the furnace room and the huge pile of chimpanzee shit. Turk kept spraying. He opened the door to the furnace room and could see the water rising higher up the pile of dung.

At work the next morning, he remembered he had a child support payment due by the end of the week. He went online to check his balances. His home equity line of credit was almost tapped out, and he was extended almost to the limit on two of his three credit cards. How had he fallen so far behind? Fortunately, he had the cushion of the $10,000 left over after his purchase of the chimps. But he was still in a precarious financial situation.

When he arrived home that evening, he had received seven traffic tickets in the mail. They were all dated during the last week of January, three weeks ago. Unknown to Turk, when the city officials had put up the stoplight, or sometime later, they must have installed a camera at the intersection. Each ticket contained a picture of Turk making a right turn from a viewpoint that included the red light and the No Right Turn on Red sign. In one of the pictures, he had raised his right hand in the direction of the sign and extended his middle finger.

There must have been a glitch in the system that had caused a delay in processing and mailing the tickets. Turk had run that red light every day, not only before but also since these citations were issued. There was no doubt that he would receive at least another twenty-one tickets in the mail. The department of motor vehicles had a point system. Once a certain number of points were accumulated, his license would be suspended. Running a red light carried a lot of points. They had the pictures. He had no defense. It would do him no good to contest the tickets. He had to have a license to drive to be able to do his job. He would have to report the loss of his license to American Security. He could lose his job.

As he backed out of his garage and into the driveway the next morning, he noticed his front door was not completely closed. It appeared that a package had been left in the front door. He got out of his car. When he opened the glass door, a large envelope flopped onto the porch. He ripped open the packet. It contained a stack of papers. On top was a summons:

> *Greetings.*
> *You have been sued …*

Liz was the petitioner, and Turk was the respondent. He turned to the next page.

Petition for Supervised Visitation

Turk went numb as he read the document.

> Upon information and belief, Petitioner has become increasingly concerned about the mental and emotional stability of Respondent and believes he poses an imminent danger to the well-being of the minor children …

> During the last unsupervised visitation that occurred in August of last year at the home of the Respondent, he exposed the children to filthy and unhealthy conditions, to wit: a huge vat full of crickets.

> Wherefore, Petitioner respectfully requests this Court order that all future visitations and parenting time be supervised by a person designated by the Court, that no overnight visits be allowed, and that no visitations take place at the residence of the Respondent until such time as the Court determines that the Respondent does not pose a significant risk to the physical, mental or emotional well-being of the minor children, that the Court set a hearing on

this matter, and that Respondent not be allowed visitation with the minor children pending the disposition of this matter.

It was five o'clock in the evening. Turk had spent the entire day at work, staring at his computer screen, immobilized. He was unable to concentrate on any task or even a specific progression of thought. How could he possibly fight the petition for supervised visitation? And how could he afford it? Would he have to prove that he was mentally fit? How would he do that? And how would he come up with the money to pay the traffic tickets? And even if he could, because of the number of tickets, he would still lose his license. And how could he survive without a driver's license for any extended period of time? As he ruminated, he made several trips to the vending machines. He drank coffee and ate donuts and candy bars.

If he lost his job, how would he be able to support himself? And how would he be able to pay child support? And if he couldn't pay child support, would they garnish his wages but then realize that he had no wages to garnish? So would they then hold a hearing and find him in contempt for not paying child support and put him in jail, where he wouldn't be able to pay support because he wouldn't be able to find a job or even temporary work because he was locked up? So would he just fall further and further behind?

He received a new email message, so he clicked on it.

Mr. Malone,

I will be at your office tomorrow morning conducting a routine audit. I will meet you at your desk at 8:30 a.m. to discuss a couple of files. You do not need to advise Mr. Smith, as he is aware that the audit is taking place.

American Security Audit Team

They must have discovered his fraudulent scheme. They must be closing in, and life as he knew it and had experienced it was coming to an end. Obviously, Smitty had to know. He had probably orchestrated the audit. Turk had thought that if this happened, which is what he had feared since the moment he deposited the check into his account, he would panic. But that was not how he felt. He was too numb to be afraid. He couldn't summon up the energy. There was too much to process. He should have known at the time that he set the scam into action that he wasn't smart enough to pull off such a scheme. He had known the risks. He had to accept defeat. His only regret was that he had lost to Smitty.

Turk stopped at the liquor store on the way home and bought a fifth of whiskey. He wasn't much of a drinker anymore, but it would be the only way to take the edge off the caffeine, blot everything out for at least one night, and maybe get some sleep before he faced the auditor in the morning.

When he got home, Bellzak was sitting at the piano, playing a song Turk had taught him, a little variation on a Chopin etude. It was not an easy piece. He was pleasantly surprised that his prodigy was doing this on his own with no expectation of getting a treat. He patted the baby chimp on his head. Turk always turned the heat down when he left in the morning. He went to the thermostat and cranked the heat back up. He filled a glass with ice. He sat down in his recliner and started chugging straight shots of whiskey.

40

Turk thought he smelled smoke. He sniffed a couple of times and then inhaled a deep breath through his nose. He felt woozy. He tried to stand up but was having difficulty pulling himself up out of his recliner. It felt so comfortable to just lie back deep into the cushions. He kicked his legs and tried to stand. He finally made it to his feet and walked to the basement door. The handle felt hot.

He opened the door, and a blast of smoke hit him in the face and overwhelmed him. He walked backward and then fell into the chair. A fog descended over his consciousness. His peripheral vision contracted.

There was a flash, and in an instant, Turk was traveling at the speed of light. He floated freely, suspended. All eternity was bound up into this one everlasting, never-ending moment.

He was an old man making love to his wife of fifty years. He was forever young in that moment. This was the first time they had ever made love. This was the moment of conception of each of their three children. This was the last time they had ever made love.

He was a soldier. He had buried a land mine just below the surface of the ground. He never knew if had killed anyone. It may have or may not have. If it did, he did not know who it was. He lived with that possibility his entire life.

He was a child who stepped on a land mine and died in an instant.

He was flying over Hiroshima, looking for traces of souls. As long as they had not been obliterated, completely blotted out from having ever existed, he could take comfort that he, too, could exist forever in this universe and beyond.

He soared over Sodom and Gomorrah. He could hear Abraham negotiating with God to try to save the city. God told him he would spare the city if he could find just ten righteous people. Maybe that was what Turk's job should have been—to try to be one of those ten people.

As he flew away, he could see on the periphery of his vision a blinding flash as God rained down burning sulfur and destroyed the city—the destruction of pure evil by pure energy resulting in a blast and a fire that cleansed the earth. Turk did not look back. The sight would have been too intense. He circled back and saw dense smoke rising like smoke from a furnace.

He was in the eye of a vast hurricane. It was heading toward land. When Earth was formed, and for millions of years, this space was empty and uninhabited. Now it was the site of a large city on a coastline where thousands of people lived. The storm continued on its path toward the city. Turk could not control it. There was nothing he could do.

His body was confined in a cell deep in the bowels of a Roman prison.

He was standing on an asphalt parking lot of a huge superstore. He could perceive that hidden and forgotten underneath was a sacred place—an Indian burial ground.

He was detained on an inpatient psychiatric unit. He had been committed involuntarily against his will. They could only hold him for three days unless a psychiatrist examined him and found that he was a danger to himself and needed to be admitted for a longer period of time.

He was the psychiatrist scanning her badge at the entrance to the unit to conduct the evaluation.

He was the father sitting in the waiting room, crying because he had done what he believed he had to do in the hope that his son would get better. He did an act out of love that he feared might cause his son to never love him again.

He was at the precipice of a black hole. He veered off to avoid being sucked into the abyss where light could be trapped and never escape. He looked back at the dark force that could never reconcile with the light. Was this where evil originated? Was there a demiurge, an evil propensity, forming in the darkness?

He came to a place called Golgotha. He could see three men hanging on crosses. There was a crowd in front of them, mocking them. Those in the crowd were faceless, except for one. That person standing in the middle was Turk. He was a witness.

He circled back to the formless dark void that was the precursor to Earth. He heard the words, "Let there be light." He passed over Eden. He could see the cherubim and the fiery sword flashing back and forth to guard the way to the tree of life.

In the next instant, the same instant, he looked up and could see the new Jerusalem descending from the sky. The dimension in which God existed was merging into the physical world, spiritualizing and transforming it into something new, both tangible and transcendent, something perfect. This was the merger of the two parallel dimensions that Felix had postulated could wipe out the need for human death and suffering. This newly created dimension would still support the existence of this and the other dimensions, and the entire universe, but there would be no more death, sorrow, crying, or pain. And Turk was a witness.

The tree of life stood in the center of the city. There would be no more night or any need of the light from the sun. Turk could see God's face and feared he might be blinded by its brilliance.

But Turk retained his vision as he stared deep into God's infinite eyes. Turk could see only the faint outline of his own reflection, but he was not afraid. All the light in the universe emanated from God's countenance. Turk did not fear that his individual soul was dissolving into the vastness of the cosmos, but he did feel that his consciousness was expanding, connecting to eternity, to God, and to the souls of others, and that his entire being—physical, mental, and spiritual—was being transformed in concert with the material world.

41

Turk rocked back in the leather chair in his office. It had been three months since the explosion. His interior wall was glass from the floor to the ceiling, so he could monitor the entire department. He was sitting at what had once been Smitty's desk. On the front edge, facing anyone who walked in, was his nameplate: William Malone, Regional Claims Manger. On the cabinet to his left was a picture of him with Liz and the kids.

His first move as claims manager had been to institute a strict no candle policy. His second executive action had been to hire a carpenter to adjust the doors to the restrooms. Now they opened outward.

He pulled a file off the top of a stack sitting on the corner of his desk. He had been auditing Crane's files. Even though Turk was now in control, that was no reason to forget, and definitely no reason to forgive, an all-out frontal attack like the one Crane had launched against him back in his claims adjuster era. Of course, he had not only defended himself but had also effectively and efficiently counterattacked with his highly developed techniques of revisionist documentation. Crane knew his job and was an asset to the company, so Turk had no plans to fire him. Still, Turk now had the power to make Crane's work life miserable, and he would continue to exact his revenge.

Crane had not contacted the claimant within twenty-four hours as required by the claims manual. Of course, no one did. That was an unreasonable standard. Crane had documented his efforts in trying to reach the guy. But Turk's new motto for the office was "No excuses, please. Results only." He furiously pounded his keyboard.

To: Stan Crane
From: William Malone, Regional Claims Manager
RE: James Sturgeon, Claim no. CF15222

What ever happened to our prompt contact policy? A full three days went by from the time this file first landed on your desk until you contacted this claimant. What if he had gone out and hired an attorney in that time? Is this the type of full service that our policyholders should expect from this organization? I suggest you reorder your priorities immediately.

Cc: Personnel File

Since his promotion, Turk had decided that ruthless efficiency was, in the end, in the broader context, the most humane way to treat employees. It gave them certainty. "Yes, Mr. Malone is an asshole," they might say, "but at least we know what is expected."

In his new position, one that he deserved and should have been promoted to long ago, he—Turk—had dominion over all these people within this dimension of his conscious perception. He could see his reflection faintly in the glass as he surveyed the office that he had reorganized in his own image. He had dropped thirty pounds. He was sleek.

Although he had been unaware at the time, when he had hosed down the basement and the drain backed up, the water had completely soaked the pile of chimpanzee shit next to the gas furnace. According to the report of the arson investigator, the shit had fermented and, in that process, had created highly flammable methane gas. The interaction of the gas and the fire from the pilot light under the furnace had set off an explosion that engulfed the entire house.

When the firefighters arrived, Turk had been found lying on the ground in the front yard, exposed to the cold on a winter night. He had been placed in an ambulance and taken to the emergency room of the nearest hospital. A question noted in the report was how had he made it from the inside of the house after the explosion and onto the front yard? Given his condition as documented in the medical records, it appeared that "smoke inhalation had rendered him unconscious and therefore unable to extricate himself from the premises."

Fortunately for Turk, and unknown to the investigators, Bellzak had been there. Turk had a vague recollection of the baby chimp turning the front door handle open and pulling him out of the house and into the front yard as the house erupted in flames.

The explosion had been the lead story on the local evening news and on the front page of the morning newspaper. But although everyone in Turk's office knew, it was not national news, and none of the executive management in the home office were aware of it.

By the time the investigation was done, there was no more interest in the story by the local television stations or newspapers. The investigator had stated in his report that he was "concerned about the discovery of the burnt remains of six chimpanzees in the basement." He noted that "Mr. Malone did not have a permit for the chimpanzees, but even if the chimpanzees had been discovered alive, it would probably only have been an infraction. And while Mr. Malone's actions were careless, they did not rise to the level of criminality and do not support a finding that he committed arson, which requires intent."

The day before the explosion, when the American Security audit investigator had wanted to meet with him, Turk had assumed it was to discuss the irregularities the investigator had found on the Mahone file and that he had discovered Turk's crime. But in fact, the investigator had wanted to meet with Turk to discuss the possible fraud they were investigating that Smitty may have committed on numerous cases, including the Mahone settlement. Turk recalled that, at the time, he had thought it unusual that Smitty had issued two checks: one to Mahone for $80,000 and a separate check for $20,000 to "Allen S. Smith, as Trustee for the Administrative Expenses Fund for American Security." Well, so had the auditors from home office.

When Turk had returned to the office after the explosion, he had met with the auditors and had done all he could to help them with their case against Smitty and to divert any attention from his own crime. And it worked. They had nailed Smitty. He had embezzled more than $300,000.

The auditor had remarked in his report how much he appreciated "Mr. Malone's efforts in aiding and assisting the investigation." So "who better to replace Mr. Smith on an interim basis, and perhaps permanently, if things work out? Mr. Malone has years of experience in handling insurance claims, and everyone in the office is familiar with him."

Turk was determined that this time he would not make the mistake he regretted earlier in his career when he had turned down a promotion so he could stay out in the field adjusting claims and not be tied to a desk in the office. And he knew all the tricks his employees might try to pull. They would not be able to outhustle the hustler.

Now that he was in control, he ran the office under his new management principles. He was considering firing two of the claims adjusters. He would be getting more done with less. He had abandoned his old philosophy of find a need and then fill that need. His new approach was to create nothing new but to take the products and services other people had created in the past, take the ways they had found to fill needs and desires, and do it cheaper and, if necessary, worse. Quality was irrelevant.

He sent a memo to all his employees that their priority should be to do their jobs and process their claims as quickly as possible. He was not concerned that they strive to improve, try to do a better job. He wanted only that they do it faster. He did not state it in the memo, but his goal was to have his staff provide as little service as possible, do as little as they could get away with, the poorer, the better, as long as it saved money. All that mattered was that they increased profits for American Security, which in turn provided them with job security and Turk with results that he could report to executive management.

These techniques were particularly well suited to managing employees. Labor costs, after all, ate into profits more than anything else. Although it was now an unrealized, and perhaps unattainable, dream, the PPP would have been the ultimate playground for this "worse is better" philosophy. But since that was no longer feasible, he would conduct his social experiments on people. And with the power of his position and little oversight from home office halfway across the country, he was in the perfect position.

The key was to treat people as replaceable, fungible commodities, much in the same way as he had once envisioned treating a world of servile monkeys. He would overwork them; train them poorly, if at all; do whatever he could to cut back on their benefits and time off; limit vacation and sick days; downsize; lay off coworkers and not replace them; provide them with little support and poor equipment; and whenever possible, fire them and replace them with less qualified people who he could pay less. Profits would soar, and Turk would move up rapidly to the top of the corporate hierarchy.

Years later, people would study how he had done it. They would write chapters in business management textbooks about it. They would teach these principles in the finest business schools across the country. The best students would get an A and become experts in how to do a lousy job. Other poor souls would get an F, fail miserably, unable to learn how to do it worse, unable to find that elusive key to controlling, and profiting, from incompetence.

Turk stared at his computer screen. He had customized the screensaver. The background was a picture of Turk's eyes that covered the entire screen. In the center, wearing a Boy Scout uniform, stood an image of Turk with his arm extended high above his head, giving the blessing he had tried to teach his chimps. He was surrounded by a huge throng of faceless chimpanzees waiving and cheering, all dressed in Boy Scout uniforms.

It was late in the evening. All his employees had left much earlier. He got up to leave. He stared at the picture of him with Nick and Alicia. He had still not seen them. He had refused to submit to supervised visitation. They were his kids. He didn't need a supervisor around. But this would all change soon. Now that he was the claims manager, he was making a lot more money, and he had fewer financial concerns. He had hired an expensive lawyer who had already filed a motion to terminate supervised visitation and sue for attorney fees for wrongfully depriving respondent of his parental rights. Turk was going to stick it to Liz and take his revenge for all the hurt she had caused him.

The lawyer had also worked out a plea bargain in which Turk got his driver's license back in exchange for paying a hefty fine. Damn, this guy was good!

Turk stared at the picture on his desk of him with his children and Liz. It was an old photo of a different place and time, and of a different person. He had placed it there to bolster his image as the perfect and responsible family man. When he looked at the photo, he knew that he had somehow survived the explosion. He knew that he was still alive now because of the pain he felt looking back at the moment captured in that picture.

And in that picture, he was smiling.

When he had awakened in the hospital, he had wondered if he had experienced a vision or had just been delusional at the time. He had been so lacking in sleep and pumped up on caffeine and sugar that he dismissed it as a hallucination or a dream, merely a manifestation, or a symptom, of his delusional state of mind.

After he was discharged, he had gone back to the ruins of his burnt-down house. On the first step to the front porch, etched in concrete, was his name, *Turk.* He searched the neighborhood and found Bellzak clinging to a tree, shivering, alone and afraid. He had brought the baby chimp to the apartment where he lived while the insurance company rebuilt his house.

He had continued to care for Bellzak in the same way as before the fire. He had bought a new piano and continued to spend countless hours teaching Bellzak how to play. After the first two months, Bellzak, the student, had far surpassed Turk, the teacher. A couple of weeks later, he had come home from work and found the door to his apartment open. Bellzak was gone. He had figured out how to unlock the door and open it. Turk had known that this could happen because Bellzak had to have been able to do this when he rescued Turk from the fire. But he had not installed a deadbolt lock because he wanted Bellzak to have free will and stay with him only if that was Bellzak's choice. Turk had not seen him since that time.

The PPP had been an utter failure, but something else had emerged from it. Driving home from the office that night, he put a disc into the CD player. At the beginning was an introduction; it was his voice. "What follows is music from a chimpanzee named Bellzak playing the piano. He is playing a piece of classical music that would be difficult for many humans to master." As the music played, Turk looked into the rearview mirror. He could see the headlights behind him and the faint reflection of his face. The pupils of his eyes were dilated and wide open, trying to perceive the light.

Turk was crying.

When he woke up the next morning, well rested and clearheaded, unlike the months and days before the explosion, he realized that in his zeal to be the head of the pack and to compensate for his flaws, he had become what he hated most. He had become Smitty. But not just Allen S. Smith. He had become Smitty on steroids!

He realized that perhaps he was wrong to have dismissed his experience after the explosion as something delusional. At the time, he had believed he had made some kind of connection, something real, something not just locked inside his brain but also at the same time infinite and extraordinary, spiritual and supernatural. He thought and therefore he was, and he thought there existed a plane of reality, or maybe a dimension, a realm of consciousness, of existence, that he was part of and that also transcended the day-to-day grind that was necessary just to stay alive.

It felt as real as anything he had ever experienced in his awake, conscious life. By not acting on what he had seen, had he screwed up the ultimate transcendental opportunity to find a need and fill that need? Had he been a witness to something yet to come, to the merger of the two parallel dimensions that Felix had described? Had he been engulfed in madness, or had he experienced a spiritual revelation? He didn't know.

Since then, and in light of what he had experienced, what had he become? How could he have strayed so far from who he truly was? Did the series of small compromises he had made in his life finally reach a tipping point that he had crossed over without realizing?

He went to his compendium of Felix's works that he had downloaded on his computer and typed in a word search for *asshole*. That seemed to fit with his recent behavior. Up popped one of Felix's treatises titled, "AAA."

> The alcoholics and the addicted in some ways
> are fortunate because they have support groups,
> others they can connect with and rely on. And they
> have specific steps that they can follow as a guide

not only to overcome their addictions but also to become better people in the process. And they are also given a guide on how they can connect to and develop a relationship with their "higher power," or as some call him or her, "God."

But those who strive for dominance, power, and control—and as part of that, of course, money— and who ultimately realize that these are false gods, they have no group they can turn to for help. They are unable to liberate themselves from the control of the parts of their brains from which their baser, primitive, animal instincts arise. They are lost in their own self-centeredness with no hope of finding a way out of themselves and the prison, the hell, in which they are trapped. That is why I have advocated for the creation of a new support group: AAA, Arrogant Assholes Anonymous.

When Turk went into the office later that morning, he sent an email to Crane telling him to meet with him in his office at nine thirty. Crane arrived exactly on time. Turk motioned for him to sit down. Crane was looking down at the floor. He did not raise his gaze to look Turk in the eye. He was a defeated man. Turk had beat him down.

"Stan, you might be wondering why I called you in here this morning," said Turk.

Crane did not look up or respond. It appeared as if he was bracing himself for something awful. He probably expected Turk was going to fire him.

"The reason I called you in here," continued Turk, "is that I want to apologize."

Crane looked up. "You want to apologize to me?" he asked.

"Yes. I wasn't happy when you called me out for that late report and copied Mr. Smith, our former claims manager. But I took it way too far, and I know that I've been making your life miserable around here. And I guess I have to admit I've been a bit of a jerk to almost everybody, but especially to you.

"And I want you to know that I won't be doing that kind of bullshit anymore. I know that you work hard and you know how to do your job and get along well with the claimants. You are an asset to this company, and I don't want to lose you. We have a great team here, and I want everyone to know how much I value each and every one of them.

"I don't know if you are aware of this, but as claims manager, I have the authority to approve spot bonuses to anyone I believe has done an outstanding job and deserves it. On your next check you will receive a $3,000 bonus on top of your regular pay as recognition and appreciation for the years of service that you have given to this company."

Crane slumped back in his chair as if he had been punched in the stomach.

"Well, Mr. Malone—"

"No. Bill," interrupted Turk.

"Thank you so much for your kind words and for the bonus. I am truly grateful," Crane said. "And I will continue to work hard and do the best I can to live up to the confidence you have shown in me."

"I have absolutely no doubt about that," said Turk. "Things are going to change around here. I'm going to institute regular meetings with all the adjusters and myself, all of us, so that we can discuss cases and collaborate and truly take a team approach, capitalizing on the knowledge, experience, and best ideas of this group of professionals."

As Crane stood up to leave, Turk extended his hand. Crane grabbed it, erupted in a huge smile, and shook Turk's hand furiously.

After lunch, Turk sent the invite for the first all-staff meeting and then called his attorney and told him to withdraw the motion to terminate supervised visitation and for attorney fees for wrongfully depriving the respondent of his parental rights.

"If we withdraw the motion, what leverage will we have?" asked his attorney.

"None. But Liz knows how important it is for her kids to have a father in their lives."

"Okay, well … what am I supposed to say to her?"

"I don't know. Will you be talking with her directly? Doesn't she have that same asshole attorney representing her, the one from the divorce?"

"No. She said she couldn't afford it."

"Tell her I miss my kids. But I'm not going to fight her anymore. I'm going to let her make the decision, and I hope she will examine her heart and her motives and come to the conclusion that supervised visitation isn't necessary. Tell her that I've changed. And please try to get the motion filed today."

A week and a half passed. It was ten thirty on Saturday morning. Turk was sitting in his apartment, reading the newspaper, when someone knocked on the door. He opened it, and Liz was standing in the hallway.

"Hi, Bill," she said. "I know I should have called first, but I've been working up the courage to do this during the entire drive down here."

"Good morning, Liz," he said. "I'm not sure what you are doing here, but I think I can safely say that I may be many things, either good or bad, but I'm not someone to be feared."

"I know. I talked to your lawyer last week and received a copy of the petition withdrawing the motion for attorney fees. I filed a petition to terminate the supervised visitation, which as you know, never actually happened because there was no visitation that occurred while the order was in effect. Fortunately, the judge was in his chambers and signed the order terminating the supervised visitation while I was waiting in the court clerk's office. Here is a copy of the motion and order for you. I wanted to give them to you personally."

"Thank you, Liz," said Turk. "Thank you very much. And just so you know, I've gotten out of the cricket business."

Liz chuckled slightly and nodded. "And congratulations on your promotion!"

"I didn't know that you knew."

"Well, information on one's ex-spouse somehow gets back. I don't know how that works."

"I already looked at the support guidelines," said Turk. "My higher salary means that I'll have to increase my support payments. And I'm fine with that. I think we can work that out ourselves. I'll pay whatever the guidelines say, and we can prepare a support modification agreement and file it with the court. We don't need to pay our lawyers three hundred dollars an hour to do that."

"I agree," said Liz. "And there is one more thing."

Turk feared that this was where she might hit him with another disappointment. This encounter had been going too well.

"Nick and Alicia are in my car in the parking lot," she continued. "I packed their pajamas and toothbrushes and all that stuff. My plan was to leave them here with you this morning. They can stay overnight, and I'll drive back down Sunday evening after dinner and pick them up. Does that work for you?"

Turk felt like he had touched an exposed electric wire and the intense jolt had jammed up the circuits in his brain. What he had hoped for and dreamed about for so long was finally right there in front of him. Was this really happening? Could this be a dream, perhaps another dream breaking through into his waking life? He didn't think so. Although he may have had some difficulty in the past differentiating between the two, he had been off of his sugar-caffeine-stimulant regime since the explosion. No, this was actually happening.

"Yes, oh yes, that definitely works for me. Yes. That works. That definitely works. And thank you so much!"

"You're welcome," she said.

"You know, and maybe I shouldn't go there right now, but at the time we separated, I told you that I thought I could change. And just so you know, I really wanted to change. I'm not sure if I could have done it, but I was willing to try, very hard, to save our marriage because whatever differences we had, I did love you."

"Changed so that you could see in the reflection from my eyes not you but the person you thought I wanted you to be?"

There was a long pause. "So did it ever work the other way?" he asked.

There was another long pause. "Bill, I don't know how to answer that question, but know this: even though our marriage is over, you were, and still are, the love of my life and the father of my children."

"You know that I feel the same way," he said. "I mean, I … I …"

"I know."

They started to reach out to each other for an embrace, as if muscle memory had taken over. Then they both stopped and withdrew. Turk might have tried to push it further, but he couldn't risk being rejected again. This was a good moment. And he would see his kids soon.

"I haven't seen Nick and Alicia for so long," said Turk. "Do they still want to see me?"

"Yes, definitely," Liz said. "Over the last year, they've asked about you many times. I sat down with them last night and told them that you had not abandoned them but that there were legal issues that were unresolved. And I told them that you loved them and wanted to see them again and be a part of their lives. And I admitted to them that I was at least partly to blame. I could have handled it better."

"And so could I," said Turk.

He grabbed Liz by the hand and started running down the hallway toward the parking lot. She kept up with him. Within moments, he would finally be with his kids again! His life with his family would probably never be the same as it had been. But all the pain he had experienced had to account for something. He believed there had to have been some meaning behind it. He could sense that he had a huge grin on his face, and he could see that Liz was also smiling. He could feel tears starting to streak down his cheeks.

It had been precarious, but for the first time he knew that he was going to make it, maybe not all the way back, but to a place he could accept. He had survived. He was going to be okay.

Printed in the United States
by Baker & Taylor Publisher Services